NURSE DIARIES

Agnes Varona Oquendo

Nurse Diaries

Agnes Varona Oquendo

DEDICATION PAGE

This book is completely dedicated to the members of my entire work family whom I have had the honor and pleasure to meet, know, love and work with throughout the span of my forty-five-year career. Teamwork, compassion, dedication and love cannot come close to describe the true medical professionals of nurses, physicians, PCAs, NAs, PAs, RTs, PTs, OTs, EMTs, CSWs, dieticians and hospital staff members that I refer to as my work family. We have all grown together, learned from each other, worked side by side of each other, lived, loved, cried, laughed and respected each other from the very beginning of our careers, during, and for some of us, up until the very last chapter. It is not and was not all so very rosy along our arduous path, but we made it work because that is who we are and most importantly what we do. Together we learned to improvise, compromise, educate, prioritize and bite our tongues because of special circumstances. I thank each and every one of you from the very bottom of my left and right ventricles for your friendship, love and guidance for well over four decades, and I hope for the next fifty decades to come. I love you all.

NURSE DIARIES

Also by Agnes Varona Oquendo:

Running Against Cancer

Agnes Varona Oquendo

My Shorts

Dark Whispers of a Serial Killer

NURSE DIARIES

Agnes Varona Oquendo

ACKNOWLEDGEMENTS

This book is only made possible because of the very special people in my life who continue to support and inspire me daily; thank you.

"One can master amazing feats when supported by glistening lights," (Agnes Varona Oquendo).

So, thank you to all of my glistening lights.

A very special thank you to:

My publisher and daughter, Lindsay Flores, who painstakingly publishes all of my work for me.

My editor and niece, Nikki Sanchez, who makes all of my work distinguishable from its original scribbled form.

My book cover photo by Anonymous, whose thought and creativity brings light and vision to my main character; nurses and an open doorway into my world.

My sister-in-law, Hilda Perez, who encouraged the creation of this book with its title.

My nephew, Charlie Clark, for your inspiration and input on Chapter 9.

To my family, The Flores Gang; Lindsay, Carlos, Leilani, Caylynn and now Reina for putting up with my inconsistent hours of working through most nights and listening to my incessant ramblings of, *"Oh, I have to sit and write. I just got a brain fart."*

NURSE DIARIES

Chapter One

Mr. Lapinsky

It has been over four and a half decades now, but I still remember it all with such a clarity as if it were just yesterday. The local hospital was about a mile away from my home. I didn't really mind the daily walk up the extremely long, gradual hill to get there, especially today on my first actual day of clinicals as a nursing student. It was the end of the summer but the start of the highly-anticipated colorful autumn season. The air was still fairly warm but fresh, as the leaves faintly begin to change from a lively deep green to a bright fiery orange as they fall freely from their summer homes. My fellow students are all sitting nervously giggling inside of the hospital lobby when I arrive. I can still feel my heart race with ambitious excitement as it competes with the butterflies swirling around aimlessly inside of my belly. We easily stood out to everyone immediately as the brand new nursing students with our pale blue and white, perfectly starched uniform dresses that purposely extend past our knees, and the stiff white nursing caps securely pinned to our heads.

We consistently carried an assignment of four to six patients for each student during the upcoming weeks of training. Our clinical instructor, Mrs. Harvey, was firm in her attempts of preparing each one of us for the real world of medicine outside of the confines of our little nursing school classroom. My assignment during the first week on the medical surgical unit consisted of four elderly patients; Mrs. Jones, diagnosed with a newly fractured right hip from a recent fall, who was impatiently awaiting medical clearance for the necessary repair of that hip fracture; Mrs. Smith was second day post-operative repair for her fractured hip; Mrs. Gonzalez was being monitored for digoxin toxicity, and of course, dear Mr. Lapinsky. I don't ever remember seeing or experiencing my own grandparents growing up, so in a sense for me during this week I had four.

Listening to each of their detailed life events was the highlight of my mornings. It fulfilled each of our needs, that I actually looked forward to arriving early every morning and getting started on my assignment. I listened with deep intensity to each of their stories as I tended to their nursing cares. But I always saved Mr. Lapinsky for last. His actual care and needs took more time to complete anyway, and he never seemed to mind waiting for me. Whenever I walked into his room, the huge smile on his face always made my entire day. I must admit, when I first laid my eyes on him, this very young nursing student felt completely overwhelmed and intimidated by his appearance alone. The tall, lean elderly gentleman lay quietly in a bed that was obviously too small for him as his feet hung just slightly over and past the mattress. His skin color appeared to take on an ashy gray hue, a color I had only read about in my medical-surgical book. A clear glass intravenous bottle hung aimlessly from a pole a few feet above his bed, and the clear tubing extended from the bottle directly into his hand, completely covered by a white, thick bulky surgical tape. The bottom half of his face from the bridge of his nose to his chin was covered by an oxygen mask with tubing that led to a huge green painted metal tank, which stood in the far corner by the head of his bed. I tried really hard not to look so frightened as I peered at him from the doorway of his single bed hospital room, ***Oh, that must be the cradle covering the bottom portion of his bed. I just couldn't picture in my head what a cradle looked like when Mrs. Harvey gave me his report. That metal apparatus fits nicely on top of the mattress and over a foot or so above his legs in a cradle shape. The top sheet and blankets are placed on top of it to prevent his bed covers from touching and putting pressure on his dressed wounds underneath. It does make perfect sense to me now that I can see it, but I wonder, is it going to be too heavy for me to remove from his bed when it is time to change the sheets? Hmm. I do see a lot of things going on in this room right now. Am I going to be able to get it all done in my time here?***

I slowly and quietly enter his room with clean linen piled up in my arms. He actually saw me standing motionless in his doorway for a few moments through his periphery vision before he began smiling at me. He immediately recognized the fear written on my face before I quickly and deliberately made provisions in my appearance by putting on my game face. I convinced myself, ***I am ready to conquer the world… or at least my patient today.*** I placed the clean linen down on top of a chair before walking over to my patient and politely introduce myself as I explain what cares I will be providing for him now. He already knew I would be caring for him. Mrs. Harvey spoke with him earlier before she made up our assignments. He carefully removed his oxygen mask and replies in a kind gentle tone,

> "It is my pleasure to meet you, Angela.
> Your nursing instructor, Mrs. Harvey, told me to expect you. She has assured me that you will be taking excellent care of me today.
> Thank you."

During this week, I actually learn a great deal from Mrs. Harvey and from each of my patients. Mr. Lapinsky was a widower and a WWI veteran. I loved listening to his storytelling as I cleansed and redressed his leg wounds. I was sure he was in a great deal of pain when I undressed his foot. The odor was undeniably unforgettable, and I secretly worry that one of his gangrenous (dead tissue) toes would fall off during the dressing change. We spoke as I worked, keeping our thoughts free from the task at my hands, as I gently remove each layer of gauze dressing wrapped neatly around his foot from the previous night. I can see the pain medication he was given thirty minutes ago is finally kicking in as he nods off in between sentences. My stomach is queasy, but my face does not give away my inner thoughts or the feeling hiding within my gut as I work quickly to redress his foot and ignore my need to scratch my itchy nose as I think, *Ah. I'm finally done. It looks pretty good, too. Nice and neat like we were taught. Good thing Mrs. Harvey had us practicing dressing changes before we actually hit the floors. I think he fell asleep too. I'll just quietly clean up everything around his bedside and let him sleep.*

I sigh to myself as I am about to leave his room and suddenly Mr. Lapinksy's surgeon enters the room and speaks quite loudly to his sleeping patient,

> "Mr. Lapinksy, how are you?
> Let me just take a look at your foot for you, OK?"

says his surgeon, as he picks up a bandage scissor from on top of the nightstand and cuts away at the dressing that I had just finished applying. I stand motionless and speechless as I watch in horror, with my mouth agape, as he unravels each and every layer of gauze.

> "It looks really good,"

says the surgeon. He then turns and looks directly at me and says,

> "You'll take care of that for me, right?"

as he quickly instructs me to redress the now exposed wound, as he practically runs out of the door. Mr. Lapinksy looks at me warmly and thinks, ***Poor thing, she just finished doing the darn thing too,*** before he says with unmistakable compassion in his voice,

> "It's ok, Angela.
> Leave it.
> The next nurse will do it."

I smile as I try to quickly redress his foot and reply calmly as I regain my composure,

> "No, no.
> I can't do that, Mr. Lapinsky.
> It's important that you have a clean dressing on your foot.
> I insist."

By Thursday I think I learned a great deal about my patients and their progress. Mrs. Gonzalez is scheduled to be discharged tomorrow, Friday morning. Mrs. Jones went for her hip repair this morning, and I will see her tomorrow when she returns to her room. I know we are taught not to become emotionally attached to our patients, but I really like my patients and feel a connection with each of them. Before leaving the unit for the day, I say goodnight to all of my patients and the nursing staff on the floor. It has become our daily ritual.

> "Goodnight, Mr. Lapinksy.
> I'll see you tomorrow."

I remember his smile as he hugs me a little longer and a little tighter than he did yesterday. I think to myself, ***He actually looks really good today. He seems very happy too, and his color isn't gray anymore***. He reaches for my hand and squeezes it in a gentle loving way before he says to me,

> "Goodbye, Angela.
> Thank you for everything.
> My children and grandchildren are coming this

afternoon to visit me.

I may be going home with them tonight.

So if you don't see me tomorrow, don't you worry, OK?

I will be just fine.

I think I should get some rest now before they arrive.

Now, you go home young lady,

and thank you again for everything.

I just want you to know that I am so happy that we met."

His eyes seem to flutter a bit before they finally close and I head home.

The next morning when Mrs. Harvey hands me my assignment, she instructs me to have a seat before she nervously clears her throat for a brief moment. She looks at me, pauses as if she needed to gather her strength first before she finally says,

"Angela, Mrs. Jones is in the intensive care unit.

Her surgery went well, but they were not able to extubate her after surgery (Removal of oral tube along with artificial ventilation).

She will probably be there for a few more days.

Sometimes this happens to someone her age.

I'm sorry... but Mr. Lapinsky expired last night in his sleep.

His family came to visit him yesterday afternoon, and then a few hours after they had left...

...The evening nurse found him deceased on her rounds.

It looks as though he went peacefully in his sleep.

I know that you were fond of him and he was very fond of you as well.

Are you alright?

It is very unfortunate that as a student nurse this has

happened to one of your patients, but it does happen.

We are taught not to get attached to our patients, but we are human, too."

I quickly wipe away my tears, and in a slightly cracked voice I say,

"Thank you, Mrs. Harvey, for telling me this before I went to his room.

I really did like Mr. Lapinsky.

I wondered why he said goodbye to me yesterday instead of goodnight before I left.

I guess he kind of knew but waited to see his family first.

He told me they were coming to see him."

Mrs. Harvey nodded her head in agreement and replied,

"That's exactly what his nurses said too.

He said goodbye to everyone yesterday; his family and the nursing staff, before he was found."

I wanted to sit and cry as I solemnly walked to his room. His few belongings were all gone as the housekeeping staff prepared his room for an admission, and my heart grew heavy with grief as I whispered to myself, ***Goodbye, Mr. Lapinsky. It was a pleasure meeting you too.***

During my first week of clinicals as a nursing student, my patients taught me so many things. I learned a compassion and empathy for my fellow human beings that cannot be found or taught through our textbooks. They taught me listening is a most valuable resource that is unfortunately used sparingly. I was seventeen at the time, and I didn't recognize that "Goodbye" was goodbye and not goodnight.

Chapter Two

Angela

Her childhood dreams are always so very clear and quite vivid in her mind. The twelve jurors are quietly seated with their hands gripping tightly onto the edge of their seats. Each juror listens intently to every single word she utters. Their eyes remain fixed upon her every move as she walks with a purpose back and forth along the corridor of the old highly prestigious looking courtroom. She communicates each and every detail elegantly with her finely chosen words. Her storytelling is riveting and painstakingly believable to her captured audience as she meticulously pleads her client's case. This was always Angela's dream, to be a trial attorney.

***

Angela is mildly startled and barely makes a move as she is awakened by the sound of her great grandchildren, as they enter the living room area where she is sitting comfortably. She pretends to have been watching her favorite show of, *Law & Order*, when she actually had been dozing off since two commercials ago. The three girls lovingly and respectfully kiss Angela's cheek as they greet her, before taking a seat beside her on the couch. ***Oh, it's my babies. Is it that time of the day already? I must have dozed off,*** thinks Angela to herself as she smiles fondly toward the three young ladies. Sisters, Carla and Lydia, are inseparable from their cousin Ellie as they chat amongst themselves. Angela listens quietly while trying to keep up with the ongoing conversation between the three young ladies. Suddenly, Carla stops talking abruptly and focuses her attention toward Angela,

"*Sorry, Mimi.*

> We really did come here to visit you.
> I don't know about them, but I want to hear more of your stories about when you were working as a nurse.
> I find them very interesting and sometimes unbelievable.
> And now that I am a college freshman, I am torn between choosing a profession in medicine or possibly law.
> I find them both intriguing.
> I think your stories and input will help guide me toward the right direction.
> So please, Mimi, tell us another story."

Lydia and Ellie smile at Carla as Lydia thinks, ***My sister Carla is always so headstrong and dramatic. So why stop now? But she truly is struggling with making a decision on her future educational plan. Ellie and I always wanted to teach, so it's a no brainer*** *for us. I have two years left before I graduate with my Bachelors in Education and then on to my Master's degree. Ellie is a freshman too, like Carla, but she already knows what her path is, unlike my sister; poor sweet Carla.* Lydia clears her throat along with her thoughts before she decides to chime in on the conversation,

> "Yes, Mimi, please tell us some more stories.
> I love listening to your stories too."

> "OK, OK, girls.
> Now let me think,"

Angela says as she crinkles her forehead while trying to think of an interesting story to tell, *Now let me see. What will be a good story to tell the girls?* Carla jumps up suddenly from her seated position on the couch and then plops herself onto the floor placing her legs into a crisscrossed position and says,

> "Mimi, tell us a crazy and wild story that happened when you were at work.
> Those are my favorites."

> "Ok then, but I think I told you this one before.
> Now let's see.
> I was working on the evening shift then, when…"

***

The temperature dropped well below freezing during the last two days. Harry Draper feels the bitter sting throughout his entire body in his desperate fight with the ongoing wind and cold wet snow burning at his face as he looks for some sort of shelter, *Shit, it's getting dark already. I have to find a place to sleep for tonight and real soon before I freeze my ass out here. Maybe I should have went south with the others,* thinks Harry, while adjusting the strap of his duffle bag that holds what is left of his entire life, resting heavily on top of his right shoulder. He carries on with the solo conversation loudly while slowly trudging through the several inches of soft fallen snow. He barely feels the quick adjustment made with the shoulder strap because of the cold dampness that invades his bones despite the several layers of clothing closely hugging his body for lack of much-needed warmth. The average looking lean thirtyish balding man has become used to living on the streets for several years now, but for some unknown reason has refused to relocate south, as some of his cohorts have done during the previous months. *What was I thinking about walking in this direction toward the beach? There's no good place for shelter over this way, just a lot of wind in this open space*, thinks Harry to himself as the snow falls harder and faster. The newly fallen snow drifts has become higher as the afternoon disappears into evening hours. Now completely frustrated with himself and the snow, Harry struggles to step off of the white blanketed hidden sidewalk and onto the street, hoping the road will be easier for him to travel along on foot.

***

    Marcus has a tight grip onto his steering wheel. He curses loudly at the windshield wipers working in full blast, *Damn things. I can't see anything out there. I guess I should have changed them like Sheila told me to last week. But like she always says, I never listen to my wife, the voice of reason.* The snow continues to fall heavily as the SUV swerves left, then right around the winding bend of road, which is now close to invisible. He thinks to himself, *Oh shit. It is snowing so hard right now. Uh, sounds like snow and hail together hitting the roof of the car out there. I probably should have left work earlier than what I did. This is what I get, but I honestly didn't think it would be this bad so fast,* then his vehicle swerves again as he tightens his grip around the wheel, covered in a soft brown leather. Out of habit, combined with his unforeseeable fear, he hits the brakes hard. The vehicle suddenly does a complete 360, sliding and skidding several times around while Marcus' fear turns to panic as his heart races in utter disbelief and uncertainty of his immediate future. He feels a slight bump in the rear of his car and thinks, *I must have hit the sidewalk curb that time. It's better than crashing into a building, I suppose,* as he struggles and fights to finally regain control of his runaway vehicle. Marcus sighs loudly, a sigh of relief as he wipes away the sweat from his forehead with the left sleeve from his gray tweed coat. His heart is still racing rapidly but a safe wave of relief immediately enters his entire realm of reality when the vehicle has finally straightened itself out. *I better slow this bad boy down. I must have been going a little too fast around that bend in my rush to get home. Alright, alright, I was going way too fast, like always,* Marcus bargains with himself as he makes the sign of the cross and now slowly heads toward home.

Harry never saw it coming. He reluctantly never even bothered to look in the direction of the oncoming traffic before he decided to step out onto the roadway. He was too busy trying to avoid facing the gusts of heavy winds striking his face with a relentless force while he carefully watches over his own footing instead, making sure not to fall. The rear end of the SUV swerved fast and hard at that very instance, making physical contact with the lean figure dressed in several layers of clothing, covered in an off-white bubble looking coat. Harry heard the loud thud before his body went flying up into the air for what seemed like a slow moving eternity before he eventually crashes head first into the huge old oak tree, ultimately halting his flight. Once in mid-air, Harry actually hears his own bones shatter, followed by a gut-wrenching pain envelope his entire frame as he thinks, *What the hell...* before everything becomes totally black. His crumpled up body made another silent thud amongst the wind as he lands awkwardly on top of a huge white blanketed snowdrift close to the tree. Never a witness to his traumatic plight, Harry lay completely still and unnoticed by all who passes by.

The snow continues to fall at the stroke of midnight as Bob skillfully backs up his ambulance into the ambulance bay of the local hospital. Charlie and Bob carefully pull the gurney out of the vehicle and rush inside of the Level I Trauma Emergency Department with their patient. The security officer manning the door nods his head to the two familiar faces before he buzzes them right in. Bob had notified the trauma team of their upcoming arrival while they were still in transit via the hospital red emergency phone. Each member of the trauma team awaits patiently on the other side of the door fully prepared and garbed from head to toe in protective gear, gowns, gloves, booties and eye-shielding masks. Emergency room surgical attending, Doug Jacobs or Dr. D, along with Chief Surgical resident Dan Chapman, grab ahold of the long board underneath the patient in unison as they assist Bob and Charlie in transferring the patient onto an emergency room stretcher from the ambulance gurney. Dr. D, quickly makes an initial assessment of the patient. He looks toward Bob curiously and says,

> "Hello, gentlemen.
> Good evening.
> What do we have here?"

Bob nods first then quickly replies,

> "We found John Doe here, unresponsive lying on top of a snowbank.
> No ID and no eyewitnesses were at the scene.
> Looks like pedestrian struck.
> Possibly a hit and run victim.
> BP 96/64, pulse 110, respirations 16, lung sounds shallow but clear, O2 sat was 89%, so we started him on 3L O2 via nasal cannula because we were unsure of his medical history.
> But he did have a pack of cigarettes in his possession.
> He does have an obvious bilateral lower extremity fracture and a left dislocated shoulder, all immobilized at the scene.
> Pupils are equal, reactive but slightly sluggish.

I don't know how long he's been out there in the snow, but he definitely has some frostbite clearly visible on all of his fingers and toes.

We placed a C-collar, started an 18-gauge IV into his right antecubital fossa with a liter of normal saline running.

We also placed another 18 gauge in his right forearm.

He looks homeless to us.

He actually awoke briefly twice.

He mumbled a few words, but we couldn't make them out.

It didn't sound like English to me, but what do I know?"

Chief surgical resident Dan Chapman has already successfully drawn and sent out several tubes filled with Harry's blood to the lab as he listens to Bob's report. The team members work efficiently and quickly in removing all of Harry's clothing, place him on a cardiac monitor, EKG obtained and read, arterial blood gasses drawn, consults called for the various departments needed even before Dr. D has finished his physical exam, as they log roll him from side to side.

Bob and Charlie quickly gathered up all of their equipment and stop at the emergency department's front desk to submit their paperwork to the staff sitting on the opposite side of the desk. Bob jumps back suddenly with the sound of a horrific scream coming from the area where they just left their patient. They quickly run back toward the screams as the team quickly responds to Harry, while he yells out in a frenzy,

"What the "F" are you all doing to me?
You can't fool me!
The secret police sent you here to kill me!
Didn't they?
Let go of me!

> Let go of me, you swine.
> Ah..., what did you do to me?
> I can't move my legs!"

Harry howls out loud in extreme pain, ***How did they find me? I must escape from my captors. I have to escape from here,*** thinks Harry while he desperately attempts to swing his right arm around before he finally loses consciousness again. The team members all sigh in relief as they release their grip from his only movable and wildly swinging extremity. Everyone looks at each other before the charge nurse blurts out calmly,

> "OK, then.
> That was very interesting.
> I guess we want to add a psych consult along with that neuro consult on this one, right doc?"

Dr. D nods his head in agreement with the nurse, then quickly replies,

> "Ah, yeah...
> Sounds right to me too.
> I'll write the order.
> OK, let's get him stabilized so we can transfer him to orthopedics service, once neuro clears him.
> Is cat scan ready for him yet?
> Are the films back yet from radiology?
> OK, let's take a look at them.
> Has anyone looked at his labs yet?
> OK then.
> Let's hang a bag of ringers lactate after we put in a central line.
> Neuro is on their way here now.
> Psych can see him up on the unit.
> I'll take care of all the admission orders now."

***

Angela yawns as she quietly walks onto the dimly lit nursing unit. From the corner of her eye she catches a glimpse of the night nurse running out of one of the private rooms located directly in front of the nurses' station. She is immediately followed by a half-filled water pitcher flying in midair across the hallway. The gold colored plastic pitcher whisks by Mary's head, barely making contact to her swaying ponytail and shoulder, as water spatters all over the newly waxed floors. Harry screams out in a frenzy as his male attendant desperately tries to calm him down,

"Get the hell out of here.
I told you to leave me alone.
Next time it won't be a water pitcher, and I assure you that next time I won't miss either.
Stupid, stupid people won't leave me alone.
Stupid, stupid, stupid."

Mary mumbles and grumbles mainly to herself as she hurriedly heads toward the sink located in the nurses' station to wash her hands. Then she grabs a few paper towels in a fruitless attempt to dry off her uniform affected by the hurling water. She smiles when she sees Angela slowly and curiously approaching the unit from the long entrance hallway leading to the nurses' station.

"Oh, good morning, Ang.
I'm so very happy to see you,"

Mary says as she disposes the paper towels into a trash can. She quickly reaches for her clipboard and nursing Kardex, (files containing all patients presently on the unit), as she takes a seat at the nurses' station desk. She quickly grabs another chair and motions for Angela to sit,

I have to hand off my patients to Ang right away. I am not letting her out of my sight until our report is over. Then they are officially her patients and no longer mine, thinks Mary to herself.

The unit secretary arrives early as usual and smiles as she tidies up her workspace for the oncoming day. Mary looks up at Ang and smiles,

> "Are you ready for report honey?
> I can tie up my loose ends after we finish report."

> "Did you have a rough night Mary?"

Angela replies as she takes the seat next to Mary.

> "Ah… yeah.
> I'm really sorry, but we assigned you our problem child.
> You are always so calm and easy going, maybe he won't give you such a hard time.
> He has a 24-hour male sitter because he is so difficult.
> But… the day shift sitter called out sick.
> They are trying to find a replacement for him.
> Let's start report on him first, then I'll give you the rest."

> "OK, Mary.
> I'm listening,"

replies Angela as she quietly listens and writes. Mary flips through the Kardex until she reaches his,

> "Harry Draper, is a 41-year old male.
> Is this your first time having him on the unit?"

Mary asks as Angela nods yes.

> "I actually requested the nursing office to send you up to us when Nancy called out sick this morning.
> This is her assignment, and it is a pretty heavy one at that.
> That's probably the reason for her sick call.
> Actually, I don't blame her at all.

OK then, back to Harry.

Day 76, he is being followed by surgical and ortho services.

He presented to the ED as an unwitnessed pedestrian struck victim.

Unconscious lying in the snow for an unknown amount of time before he was eventually found.

He is status post healed bilateral tib/fib (Tibia/Fibula) fractures and a left dislocated humerus.

Well, a long story short to this scenario is...

He's homeless with obvious psychological issues going on.

He now has several necrotic toes from lying in the snow, an obvious outcome of frostbite.

They need to be amputated, but he is refusing.

He is also refusing dressing changes to his feet.

He is pretty much refusing almost all cares, medication and treatments prescribed for him.

Sometimes he goes off on some conspiracy theory he has and he honestly believes.

We are waiting for a response of a court order to remove the necrotic tissue from his feet because of the possibility of him becoming septic.

He has been stopped by security several times while on this unit attempting to elope, so now he has 24 hour sitters, preferably all male.

He does seem to respond more favorably to males rather than women in general.

I think he's kind of intimidated by male authority figures and has no respect for women.

He needs IV antibiotics, but he refuses to keep a line in.

He has ripped out several already, and he occasionally will accept his oral medications.

I guess it all depends on his mood.

But be very careful.

He is verbally abusive to the nursing staff, and he can be physically combative as well.

He is very impulsive and extremely short tempered.

Girl, I wish you luck with him.

You are certainly going to need it.

You saw how he threw me out of his room this morning, then tossed his water pitcher at me,

and that isn't the worst of what he has done.

The water did hit me; his aim isn't half bad.

He will throw anything within his reach at you.

Now let me give you report on your other five patients, then I have a few more meds to dispense, finish up all of my nursing notes and then I'm out of here, finally.

It's been a long stressful night for me, and I am exhausted."

Angela mentally prepares herself for the day ahead of her by planning her strategy as she listens to Mary talk, *I'll check my doctor's orders first, then make rounds and do my vital signs, along with my patients assessments and blood glucoses all together. Then I should pour my meds, administer insulins, hang new IV bags, stock my supplies for the day, pass meds with breakfast. I should have all of that completed so that I can attend surgical rounds, medical rounds, and then social service rounds. I want to make sure to help the nursing assistants with my patient's cares, and then we can do Mr. Draper together, do some charting and get a quick coffee break in there somewhere. OK, that should work if nothing unexpected happens in between, then I'll have to modify it all over again. OK, let's do this Angela.*

Angela works quickly and efficiently throughout the morning, staying on her proposed mental schedule. She looks at her nursing assistant Mandy and says,

"Are you ready?

Let's go and take care of Mr. Draper together.

His sitter Oliver is in there with him.
He came in for overtime and he is really good with Harry.

I peaked in a few times, and they were playing cards.

He's calm.
It's a good time for us.
We can do everything we need to do quickly and keep him calm at the same time."

Mandy nods her head in agreement with Angela and replies,

"OK, let's do it then.
I think working together is a great idea.
Thanks, Ang."

The two women enter Harry's room with hidden caution but with an air of confidence and needed supplies inside of a plastic bag. Angela smiles at Harry and Oliver and says in a soft calm voice,

"Good morning, gentlemen.
How are you feeling this morning, Harry?
Mandy and I are going to make your bed and get you some fresh water.
Is there anything you need for today Harry?"

Harry looks at Angela curiously at first and then replies as he crinkles his forehead,

"I recognize you.
I have seen you before.
But you have never taken care of me up here in this room, right?"

"You are absolutely right Harry.
I am a float nurse.
I work everywhere in the hospital, wherever they need me for the day.

> I was working in the emergency room the evening you arrived.
> I was one of the nurses who cared for you that day,"

Angela answers Harry's questions honestly, as she and Mandy work quickly to complete the needed tasks at hand. She recalls that very evening she worked in the ED when Harry was brought in, *My God, he was a mess. At first he just moaned in pain as we quietly worked in unison, quickly cutting away at his clothing as team leader, Dr. D, assessed him and verbally gave orders. Everyone worked quickly to save Harry's life. It was absolutely amazing working alongside my colleagues. Everyone had a job and everyone's role was conducted as if it were practiced minutes ago. Such an amazing team, and I remember it just as if it were yesterday.* Oliver has worked with Angela many times throughout the years and had already completed the vital signs on Harry as she requested of him earlier. Angela was able to give a quick report to Oliver before he initially entered Harry's room.

> "OK, Harry.
> We are done here,
> but I am going to change the dressings on your feet.
> That is really important."

Harry looks up from his cards and replies to Angela,

> "Thank you,
> but I already changed the dressings to my feet myself just before Oliver arrived.
> I like to take care of them myself.
> I know how to do it.
> I used to watch the doctors do it."

Angela calmly looks toward Harry as she observes his body language and facial expression before she says,

> "Oh, that's is great Harry.
> Can I take a look at your work?

I also need to document the progress of your wounds.
If they have already healed, then we won't need to
continue with the dressing changes anymore."

Harry looks at Angela curiously for a brief moment, then he immediately shifts his attention toward his feet before he carefully chooses his words and states,

"I'm really tired right now.
I'll let you change the dressings after lunch.
OK?"

"OK then, Harry.
I'll be back after lunch.
Can I do anything else for you now?"

"No, no, no.
Oliver can help me with anything I may need until you come back.
Thank you, nurse."

Mandy scans Harry's room, then adds,

"Harry, I'll bring you back some fresh water.
But where is your water pitcher?"

Harry smiles and giggles before he replies,

"Oh...
I guess the night nurse forgot to bring me back my
pitcher.
No ice, please."

"OK Harry.
I'll get you a new one.
Be back in a few minutes,"

Mandy replies as she follows Angela out of the room. Angela quickly documents on Harry's chart in anticipation of having to add another nurse's entry in his chart after lunch, *Will he let me change his dressings as he promised, or will he give me hard time? We shall see,* thinks Angela to herself.

Chief surgical Resident Dan Chapman, along with his surgical team, gather in a circle at the entrance of the unit in the far end of the long hall discussing and reviewing a letter held in Dan's hands. *Hmm… We already did surgical rounds earlier. I wonder what is going on over there?,* thinks Angela as she looks curiously toward the team before passing out her noon meds. Dan sees Angela and waves at her in a motion to come and join them. He meets her halfway in the hall, puts his arm around her shoulder and asks,

"Did Harry let you change his dressings today?"

"No, he didn't.
He said I can do it after lunch.
Why?"

Dan shows her the letter he received from the court.

"We just received this court order allowing us to treat him even if he refuses.
I am interested as to what Harry's reaction is going to be when I show him this paper.
We will change his dressings today.
We need to assess his wounds and decide how his wounds should be treated.
Can you gather up all of the supplies for a dressing change for us?
We'll need a debridement tray, suture removal kit, sterile containers, lidocaine, syringes, sterile gloves and gowns, culture swab sticks, and his PRN pain medication.
And anything else you think we may need.
I'm not sure what is under those dressings of his."

"Sure.
I'll get it all ready for you now.

Just give me fifteen minutes,"

Angela replies as she makes her way back to the nurses' station.

***

Dan enters Harry's room, followed by his surgical team. An intern, Harry's intern, Dr. Samantha Clarke, addresses her patient. She then turns her attention to the team by reviewing Harry's medical/surgical history, recent laboratory findings and plan of care. Oliver and Harry listen quietly to the surgeons' conversation as they hover around Harry's bed. Dan refocuses his attention from his surgical interns and residents to Harry and inquires,

"Harry, how are you feeling today?
Has the nurses changed your dressings yet?"

Harry smiles and shakes his head no before he replies,

"She is coming back this afternoon to change them."

Dan hesitates a moment as he searches for words that will not set Harry off into one of his rages, something he is known to do quite often. He clears his throat first, then continues,

"So here is the thing, Harry.
I know that you have been refusing to allow the nurses to change your dressings for some time now.
Dr. Clarke has explained to you countless times the importance of this procedure.
We need to take a look at your feet right now.
So we are here to change your dressings now, Harry."

Samantha begins to don a yellow protective gown and gloves as her colleagues drapes a bedside table with a sterile towel. Then they prepare the sterile field with sterile supplies for the dressing change. Harry sits quietly and stares at the doctors as they work, *Shit, they have just ganged up on me in my own room. It is going to be fun seeing their reactions when they remove my dressings from my feet,* thinks Harry before he deliberately states in an eerie but calm manner,

> "What if I refuse?"

> "You can't refuse any longer, Harry.
> I have a court order right here that states, *you cannot refuse any longer.*
> Psychiatry and the other department heads has helped us in getting an approval from the courts.
> It is a necessary procedure in keeping you healthy, Harry.
> We have discussed this numerous times with you,"

Dr. Chapman pleads with Harry as he flashes the envelope in front of him. A devious grin immediately transforms over Harry's face before he belts out a brief roar of laughter. He then lays back comfortably in his bed and blurts out loud,

> "Go ahead pagans.
> Do what you will with me!
> You may be able to take control of my flesh right now, but never will you dominate my mind.
> Never, never, never!"

Everyone in the room had grown used to Harry's unusual behavior as each person thinks to themselves, *Harry has always been eccentric and unusual in every possible way, but this behavior is over the top even for Harry. He is definitely up to something, but what?* One of the interns, Dr. Joe Olsen, begins cutting away at Harry's very old crusted gauze dressings after placing a blue absorbency pad under Harry's feet to protect his bed sheets from the drainage. As he comes closer to the bottom layers of gauze, he can see old dried blood causing the gauze to stick to Harry's feet. Another intern instinctively pours normal saline over the sticking gauze, as the smell of dead tissue becomes more and more evident to everyone in the room. Harry continues to smile as his attention moves from face to face to face, watching the expressions on the doctors faces and then to Oliver. Joe thinks to himself, *I'm glad that I put on a surgical mask before I began cutting away at his dressings. Hmm, he doesn't seem to be in any pain or discomfort over this dressing change. He actually seems to be enjoying himself. Definitely a strange reaction from him. Hmm, I wonder,* as he waits a few minutes for the saline to soak its way into the gauze. Joe then begins slowly pulling the gauze away, careful not to yank the dressing off. He remembers about a month or so ago almost being kicked in the face by Harry when he tried to remove the dressing too quickly from his feet as he thinks, *I think this looks like the dressing I put on him a month ago. No, it can't be that long ago since he let someone change his dressings, can it be?* Once the final layer is finally removed, initially not a word is spoken. *The smell is quite horrific,* thinks Oliver to himself, but he dares not to say a word aloud. Harry relishes over each and every one of the facial expressions displayed throughout his room. Dr. Chapman breaks the silence and asks,

> "Harry, where are your toes?
> No one has ever charted or reported that any of your toes had fallen off.
> It's impossible that all ten of them are gone now."
> They were all in different stages of gangrene.
> Harry, what happened here?"

Harry smiles, then grins widely before he lets out a menacing sound of laughter. He then calmly replies,

> "I'll never tell."

Dan clears his throat and thinks to himself, *His toes did not fall off by themselves. The remaining tissue looks grossly infected. There's quite a bit of purulent drainage. Harry what did you do?,* before he adds,

> "OK, then.
> Someone take a picture of his feet for his chart.
> Harry, we need to document your progress into your chart.
> A picture says it all.
> Samantha, after the pictures are taken, clean and dress his feet, please.
> Harry, we are going to send you for some radiologic procedures when we are done here.
> It's just a precaution and hospital protocol.
> Oliver, can you transport him to radiology when she's done?
> Joe, do you mind going with Oliver?
> Make sure they get some good films, Joe,"

Dan says as he looks straight into Joe's eyes. Joe nods his head before he discards the old gauze dressing, removes his gloves and then washes his hands as he waits for Dan at the nurses' station. Joe looks up as he sees Dan leave Harry's room and walk towards the sink inside of the nurses' station. After Dan washes his hands he places a call to radiology. Dan turns his head to Joe and says,

> "Keep him down there.
> We are gonna search his room while he's in radiology.
> Between the x-rays, doppler studies and sonography I have ordered, we should have a clearer picture of what we have just witnessed.
> I have a funny feeling in my gut about this whole thing.
> I'll beep you when we are done up here."

Once Dan sees the gurney leaving Harry's room, he and the remainder of his team reenter the room. Samantha curiously looks at Dan first and asks him,

"What are we looking for, chief?"

"I don't really know Sam,
but when we do find it, you will know it.
Everyone, just search everywhere.
I have a feeling Harry amputated his own toes.
It really wouldn't surprise me if he did.
Most of his actions are really quite extreme and bizarre."

Dan looks around the room as he thinks, *OK now. Try and think like Harry. Where would Harry hide something to keep it safe? Hmm.* Dan looks under the bed and thinks, *He must not let housekeeping clean under here either, it's a bit dusty.* Then his gut tells him to look up at the ceiling tiles, *I wonder...* Dan quickly grabs a chair from the corner of the room. He takes a deep breath before he makes the decision to stand on it and slowly pushes away at one of the off white ceiling tiles. Dan let's out a horrifying scream as something small brushes down along the side of his face and shoulder before it lands on the floor beside the chair, *No... Did a necrotic toe just touch my face?* Everyone stops in the middle of their individual search to take a long hard look at what is actually lying on the floor. Dan quickly removes his examination gloves. He replaces them with a pair of sterile gloves before reaching down onto the floor. With his thumb and index finger, he gingerly picks up a completely blackened great toe. He then raises the toe to his eye level and examines it closely before he places it into a sterile plastic container held open by Samantha. *I bet the rest of his toes are up there too,* thinks Dan and everyone else in the room. Dan and one of his first-year interns search the remaining ceiling tiles, finding nine more stray toes along with bandage scissors and a Kelley clamp. Each toe is then carefully placed into its own sterile specimen container, properly labeled with Harry's name, room number, hospital ID, body part and sent to the pathology lab for testing to either confirm or discredit their findings. Dan thinks to himself, *I can't wait to see that pathology report.*

***

Angela smiles at her girls. She recognizes the look of anticipation written on their faces. Carla shifts her position. She closes her mouth once she realizes her mouth is wide open, thinking, *That is such a good story, maybe a little gross but good,* and responds by saying,

> "But what happened to Harry?
> Please tell us.
> We have to know what happens next."

> "Well, Harry had his fun with us all, but he eventually agreed to be treated.
> Once he was completely recovered from all of his physical injuries, he really wanted to leave the hospital.
> But because he was homeless, social services had to find a place for him to be discharged to.
> We couldn't ethically discharge him back out into the street.
> But after a few months of searching, they finally did find a group home that would accept him out of state.
> After he was eventually discharged from the hospital, I don't know what ever became of him,
> but I will never forget him, that is for sure."

Chapter Three

Was it a Murder?

Andy Chase is a completely miserable man. His wife left him several years earlier and life just kept getting worse as the years passed by. Now, he sits impatiently in the emergency room waiting for test results. He contemplates as he waits, *Why, why, why does everything happen to me? I must be getting one of those new crazy diseases that leave you helpless and paralyzed. When are they coming back in here to tell me something? Anything? They just leave you in one of these freezing cold rooms and then they forget all about you; that's what they do. They did the same exact thing to me last week at the other hospital, too.* Emergency room attending, Dr. Jeff Carter, walks into room number 6, a small examination room within the emergency department. He is accompanied by an emergency room nurse, as he addresses Andy seated upright on top of the examination table in his drab non-descript hospital gown,

> "Mr. Chase, there is obviously something neurological going on here.
>
> We would like to have you admitted and run a few more tests.
>
> We have consulted with neurology and will have you admitted under their services."

"OK, but what is exactly wrong with me?

My legs are getting weaker and weaker by the second.

I need some help here.

Soon I won't even be able to walk at all, and I won't be able to take care of myself any longer either.

I can't live like this."

Dr. Carter pauses and sympathizes with Andy before he replies,

"We are not sure yet, Andy.

That is why we would like for you to undergo further testing so that we may be able to give you a more definitive answer to your questions."

"But what do you think it is, Doc?

I was thinking maybe I have MS or multiple sclerosis?

Definitely a debilitating disease, I think.

I have been doing some research on my own.

Could that be it doc?"

"That could be a possibility, Andy.

But as I suggested, we need to do further testing before we can make that diagnosis, sir.

Now, let's get you admitted first.

Nurse Regina here will help get you admitted to the neurology unit."

***

Andy smiles and lets out a satisfying sigh to himself as he changes television stations on the small personal television set directly in front of him. *This room is actually not so bad after all. I really wanted a private room, but the nurses haven't given me a roommate yet for several days now. My room is bright, clean and at the end of the hallway far enough away from that noisy nurses' station. I don't even have to cook for myself as long as I am a hospitalized patient. It is all so very good, as far as I am concerned. The nursing staff is fairly pleasant, and they don't bother me at all. A win, win situation for me, is how I look at it. I don't even mind all of the tests they have been putting me through.*

Nancy walks into Andy's room with a smile on her face as she hands him his medication,

> "Here are your morning meds, Andy.
> I also have two pain pills in there for you,
> just like you requested earlier.
> Is there anything else I can do for you before I leave?"

Andy swallows his medication in one big gulp before he answers,

> "No, no, I'm good for now, Nancy.
> If you can just bring in my next pain pills right after lunch, that would be great.
> This way the pain won't get worse.
> We'll nip it right in the butt that way."

Nancy smiles as if that smile was permanently drawn onto her face. She accepts, then discards the used small medication cup into a small trashcan before replying,

> "Andy, it is still a PRN medication,
> or given as needed.
> I explained that to you yesterday, remember?
> You have to request it when you need it."

Andy frowns before he says,

> "Oh, yeah.
> That's right.
> I'll ask my doc to change it to ATC, around the clock, when he comes in today."

"Oh, by the way, Andy,

the bed next to you is the last open bed we have on the unit,

so you will be getting a roommate sometime today."

"What?

I should be in a private room all by myself.

If I share my room with someone else, they could make me much sicker than what I already am.

My immune system is so very weak.

I could catch whatever he has.

You need to put me into a private room right away Nancy,"

Andy pleads with his nurse. Nancy listens with compassion to her patient and replies calmly,

"Andy, I assure you, we would never put your health at risk.

I cannot tell you what is wrong with the gentleman being admitted today, you know, HIPPA and all,

but what I can tell you is that you cannot catch anything he has.

We have already considered his and your health issues before making this decision.

You will be just fine, Andy."

"OK then.

I suppose I don't really have a choice in this matter, do I?

But as soon as a private room does becomes available, it's mine, right?

Just remember, I am not happy with the idea of having a roommate.

In fact, I am really worried about it."

"OK, Andy, it's noted,"

Nancy answers Andy before she leaves his room.

***

The emergency room transporter assists Nancy and her nursing assistant transfer, Salvatore Mason, from the emergency room gurney onto his semi private room bed situated closest to the door. After making her newest patient comfortable and completing his admission assessment along with some of her paperwork, she pulls open the curtain from around Salvatore. Nancy quietly peeks around the curtain toward Andy and thinks, *Hmm, his eyes are closed. Perhaps he is asleep or maybe he is just pretending to be. Well, whatever it is, I hope he will behave himself*. She then decides it is best to keep the curtain drawn between the two men for now and without making a sound, she leaves the room.

Nancy passes out her afternoon medication, makes her rounds, then eventually sits inside of the nurses' station to complete her admission paperwork and patient charting. *Ah, let's see now,* thinks Nancy as she writes. *Salvatore Mason is an alert ninety-year-old lean male with periods of forgetfulness and confusion. Diagnosis; oxygen dependent COPD, renal insufficiency and status post fall with a pelvic fracture admitted from a skilled nursing facility. Oxygen 2L via nasal cannula in place, urine catheter intact, and patent draining cloudy yellow urine, KVO (keep vein open) IV intact and healthy to right forearm. OK, orders transcribed, and my paperwork is all done. I guess in the morning Andy will give me a full report about his night and his opinion of how his new roommate behaved as well,* thinks Nancy as she prepares to give her report to the oncoming shift.

***

The next morning, after receiving report from the night-shift nurse, Nancy makes her early morning rounds and looks in on Andy and Salvatore first as she remembers what the nurse told her, *She had to get a doctor's order for a sleeping pill for Salvatore. Oh, I'm sure Andy will tell me all about his night.* She quietly opens the door and tiptoes inside of the room. *Oh good, they are both sound asleep,* then she quietly steps out and continues making her rounds before passing out her early medications. Nancy hears the all too familiar sound of a patient call bell buzzing. Then after several minutes she observes her nursing assistant walking towards her saying,

> "Nanc, Mr. Chase would like to see you.
> He said to bring his pain medication in with you, too."

> "Oh, OK, thanks, hun.
> Did he say what he wanted, by any chance?"

> "No, Nancy.
> He just said he wanted to talk to you, that's all."

Nancy quickly administers her early morning insulins to her two diabetic patients, then pours Andy's medication before she walks down the hall and enters his room. She takes a long deep cleansing breath first as she anticipates a long list of Andy's concerns.

> "Good morning, Andy.
> How was your night?
> I was in earlier but you were asleep, and I didn't want to wake you."

Andy looks up at his nurse and frowns before he eagerly replies to Nancy,

> "Well, it was certainly a very long night.
> Sal is I'm sure a very nice guy, but he was moaning most of the night.
> So, we both didn't get very much sleep.

I think his sleeping pill finally kicked in at about three this morning, or at least that is when he finally fell asleep.

I hope tonight is not a repeat performance of last night.

Is anyone being discharged today from one of the private rooms?

`Cause now I am behind in my natural sleep pattern.

In fact, it is completely disrupted."

Nancy hands over the little cup to Andy containing his medication. She stands by and watches as he first counts his pills, *Four, five, six, seven,* then tosses them all at once into his mouth, followed by a small chug of water, then says,

"All gone.

Now what about that private room?"

"Sorry, not today, Andy.

No one is being discharged from one of our private rooms.

If you like, I can check and see if another unit has an available private room,

but I cannot make any promises."

Andy frowns his forehead again as he contemplates Nancy's offer and replies,

"I guess we can wait another day or two and see if one becomes available here.

I don't want to have to get used to a whole new set of nursing staff again."

"OK, then, Andy.

We can do that."

Nancy says as she discreetly walks over to Salvatore. She wraps the blood pressure cuff around his left upper arm to recheck his blood pressure as she makes a mental assessment of his overall physical condition and asks,

> "Good morning, Mr. Mason.
> How are you feeling this morning?"

Nancy says as she checks his radial and pedal pulses while she speaks to him. Then she listens to his heart and lung sounds before she instinctively shifts her stethoscope to his abdomen, checking for bowel sounds. Salvatore answers her in a low, whispery voice,

> "I'm OK, nurse.
> Just a little bit tired, that's all."

> "I see.
> Would you like something for pain?"

Salvatore slowly opens his eyes to look up at his nurse and smiles at her friendly face,

> "No, thank you.
> I only have pain when I move.
> I don't plan on moving right now, nurse,"

Salvatore says as he takes a hold of her hand and gently squeezes it.

> "OK, Mr. Mason.
> I will bring you in a pain pill in about a half hour or so.
> This way my nurse's assistant and I can help you get freshened up for the day.
> It will help you to feel better.
> We will have to turn and move you around a bit, but we will be gentle.
> I promise."

Salvatore smiles again and replies,

> "You can do whatever it is you need to do.

>I'm confident that you know what is best for me.
>In case I forget, nurse, thank you for everything."

Nancy returns his smile as she feels a warmness envelope her entire heart. She suddenly finds herself squeezing his hand back for over several seconds before she leaves the room and hurries down the hallway trying not to miss neuro rounds.

After spending a week with his roommate, Andy demands to be placed into a private room on any unit, *If I wanted a roommate, I'd get myself another wife. This is ridiculous. My roommate is preventing me from recovering like I should. I'm sure I'm gonna catch whatever it is he has soon. Of course they aren't gonna tell me the truth about that. They just want to keep all of the beds occupied to make money. I've had enough already. He gets confused every evening, and then the moaning starts. That damn moaning lasts all night long. Now how am I supposed to get my rest with all of that noise he makes? I can't live like this anymore.*

The night nurse, Olivia, makes her rounds as she dispenses her midnight medication. Instinctively, she follows the sound of Salvatore moaning before she enters his room. Olivia tries to comfort Salvatore by repositioning him first before administering him his pain medication. ***Poor thing. Between his physical injuries, his Alzheimer's dementia and sundowning, he is just so miserable,*** thinks Olivia to herself. Andy listens intently to everything happening on the other side of the drawn curtain and yells out to the nurse,

>"Did he even have his sleeping pill yet?
>If he didn't, can you give him two pills, please?
>Maybe he will get some sleep then,
>and then maybe I can finally get some sleep, too."

After hearing Andy speak, Olivia sighs and rolls her eyes as she thinks, ***Good thing he can't see me through this curtain. He is always complaining about something or someone. It is so sad; he is never happy about anything, ever.*** Olivia clears her throat, takes a deep breath and answers Andy calmly,

"Oh, Andy, I'm so sorry.
I just gave him some meds, he should fall asleep soon.

Would you like a sleeping pill too?
You do have one already ordered, if you need it."

"Ah… OK.
I'll take one."

"OK, Andy.
I'll be right back with it."

When Olivia returns with a sleeping pill for Andy, she is relieved to see that Salvatore is asleep and quiet.

By three a.m., Olivia finally sits down behind the nurses' station as she mentally reviews her assignment and thinks, *OK now. I did the wound care in Rooms 606 and 609. My meds are all done for now, admission assessment is done, patient rounds are done, new IV bags are hung, needed supplies for the morning are all ordered. So now I can sit and start on my nurse's notes, complete my admission paperwork, and do my 24-hour chart checks, (check all of her patients' charts for written doctor's orders over a 24-hour period and confirm that the orders have been carried out). I better get moving while it's still "Q."* Nurses generally never refer to their current shift as being quiet. It usually leaves an uncanny bad taste in the staff's mouth once the shit has hit the fan, then all kinds of craziness begins to occur in succession or simultaneously. It is probably worse than the effects of a full moon on patients.

Olivia takes a quick glance up at the wall clock across from the nurses' station as she makes her last nurse's note entry. *Oh, I think that I better get an early start on my morning med pass. I just may get out of here on time this morning. It looks as though I'm all caught up,* Olivia smiles at that pleasant thought. *Geez, I can't remember the last time when I actually left work on time. Oh, now I remember, never!* She walks lightly down the dimly lit hallway with an IV antibiotic bag in her hand, scheduled for one of her patients. Her nursing and maternal instincts are gnawing at her curiosity, so she decides, *I think that I better go and look in on Salvatore first.* Olivia slowly pushes open the door fully to his room. She had purposely left it open at just a crack, a few hours earlier. The light coming from the hallway alone allows her to see Salvatore's shadow sitting upright in his bed as she tiptoes closer toward him. A frightening feeling immediately creeps up from inside of her stomach as she thinks, *Something looks funny here. My gut tells me that something is not right with this picture.* Olivia instinctively stands up tall onto her toes and reaches over the head of Sal's bed to pull the cord from his overhead light. Her eyes quickly makes the adjustment from darkness to light. She blinks her eyes quickly, again trying to focus on the sight before her. Suddenly Olivia gasps in horror. She drops the IV antibiotic bag from her hand onto the floor, making a light thud. She feels a wave of panic, then nausea rush through her entire body as she reaches toward the wall pressing the red code button. Then she runs to the doorway yelling out loud, *"Help, Help, Help!"* Her colleagues on the unit all run towards her voice, followed by the hospital's code team. Olivia stands outside of Sal's room, all color completely drained from her paled face as tears flow freely from her eyes. The medical resident and interns on call for the night gently move Olivia out of their way as they dash into the semi-private room.

The entire team freezes in mid motion as they move inside of the room one by one. The medical resident, Nick, stares at Salvatore briefly and whispers in a low but audible voice, *What the hell happened in here?* He then sees the nursing supervisor enter the room and says to her in a calm but obvious shocked tone in his voice,

"I think… you better call 911.
This is going to be a M.E. (Medical Examiner) case for sure."

The supervisor takes a quick shocking look at Salvatore, nods her head in agreement, and makes her way to the nurses' station to make that call. Nick immediately walks over to Salvatore, checks for a pulse; *none.* He knows what the outcome is, but he listens for a heartbeat anyway with his stethoscope; *nothing.* All eyes in the room are glued onto Nick. Not a word is spoken as everyone stands frozen. Nick thinks for a quick moment and decides they should wait for the police to arrive. He instructs the team to return to their units and only those directly involved with the patient, himself and the nursing supervisor, should stay and wait for the police. He sadly looks at Salvatore and thinks, ***Who did this to you? Who would suffocate this elderly gentleman? Or better yet, what kind of person would do this to another person?*** He dared not to touch the plastic bag. Nick stands reasonably far enough away as he inspects the bag that seemed to be placed meticulously around Sal's head. ***Hmm, whoever did this, tied it fairly tightly around his neck, disallowing any possible entry of much needed air. His lips and nailbeds are obviously cyanotic, (blue due to insufficient oxygenation). His oxygen cannula is conveniently laying on the floor. This all probably happened about an hour or so ago, I'd say, or just after the nurse made her rounds. Hmm, I wonder,*** thinks Nick as he gently peeks onto the other side of the curtain. ***His roommate appears to be asleep. I wonder. Hmm, I wonder.***

***

Carla sits straight up quickly changing her position from lying on her stomach on the floor with her arms propped up holding her head up under her chin. Her eyes are wide with horror and curiosity rolled up into one,

> "But Mimi, but Mimi,
> what happened to Salvatore?
> I mean, who tied the bag around his head and neck?

Who did this?"

Mimi smiles before she answers Carla.

"Well, I don't know for sure.
The police came and investigated the crime.
They interviewed the entire night staff and everyone who ever cared for Salvatore and Andy.
The nursing and medical staff were completely dev-
astated by this very traumatic event.
Everyone suspected it was his roommate Andy,
but I don't know what was eventually concluded by
law enforcement.
Once patients are discharged from the hospital, we
rarely find out what happens to them unless they are
readmitted.
I heard Andy was discharged the next day,
but that is all I know.
It was a very unusually bizarre, sad thing that had
happened a very long time ago.
Actually, I don't even recall reading about it in the
newspaper, either."

Carla looks at Angela as she tilts her head down to the left and
then to the right in her confusion before she asks,

"What is a newspaper?"

Chapter Four

The Runner

Angela thinks long and hard about the last two stories she just shared with her granddaughters. She comes to the conclusion, *I don't want them to think that the medical field is always so grim and depressing, because it's really not. In fact, it can be predictable and unpredictable, but yet rewarding and so damn frustrating as well*. She thinks back trying to remember another type of story and scenario to share with them.

"You know girls,
the medical field can be so many things for so many different people.
It can be responsible for unleashing so many different emotions in a person.
Sometimes it can be really scary or rewarding and gratifying.
It can also be very sad, or happy or exciting, and even so, so much more.
I remember a case when I was a very young nurse.
I took care of this man...

***

Hector Vazquez exits from the center of several elevators and walks up onto the medical surgical unit from the admitting office. Accompanied by his wife and a hospital volunteer, his nervousness goes undetected by most onlookers. The volunteer drops off paperwork at the nurses' station before showing Hector to his room, a semi private room located directly across from the nurses' station. His primary nurse, Angela, walks into his room a few moments later as she cordially introduces herself to her newest patient.

"Hello, Mr. Vazquez.

My name is Angela, and I am your nurse this morning."

Angela looks over Hector's paperwork first, left by the volunteer, as she begins filling out his admission papers after recording his vital signs.

"Ok, Mr. Vazquez, I see that you are scheduled for surgery in two days."

"Yes, Angela.

I have a brain tumor.

My doctor has scheduled me for a few tests and bloodwork first before my surgery.

He says that I am very lucky because it was found early."

Hector smiles, hiding the fear sitting in the depths of his soul as he continues to answer all of Angela's questions. Angela listens carefully while she writes and thinks, *He looks so healthy. My God, he's only thirty-five. He's also athletic and married with young children. Why? His MD orders do include pre-operative bloodwork, EKG, chest x-ray and Cat Scan. OK, we are almost done here. Oh, they are here already to do his EKG. I can finish this paperwork up later.*

"OK, Mr. Vazquez.

This nice young lady over here is Paula.

She is going to do an EKG on you.

It is part of your pre-op testing for your surgery."

Angela says as she points towards Paula.

"I will be back when Paula is all done.

Your doctor wants me to start an IV on you as well."

"OK, Angela, thank you,"

Hector says nervously as he nods his head in agreement. He stares ahead at a poster of himself crossing the finishing line of a local race pinned up on the corkboard facing his bed. For a very brief moment he mentally prepares himself for all of the testing and ultimate pending brain surgery ordered by his physician, *Am I ready for all of this? He is actually going to cut open my skull to get to my brain. I know that I am strong but… That picture of me breaking tape at the finish line is just a reminder for me of just how strong I really am. Funny, in a sense, all of the races that I have ran and completed are just a dress rehearsal for this next very big race of my life. Yes, the biggest race of my life*, thinks Hector to himself as he smiles. He then looks up at the ceiling and makes the sign of the cross with a brief prayer to himself.

On the morning of Hector's scheduled surgery, Angela arrives early to the unit. She thinks to herself as the elevator door opens, *I know Mr. Vazquez is scheduled as an early case, either first or second. I hope I make it in time to wish him luck before he leaves the unit for pre-op.* As she is about to enter her floor, she can see an operating room stretcher slowly approaching her. Once it is closer, she can clearly see Mrs. Vazquez walking alongside of the gurney. Steve, the operating room transporter, stops in front of Angela before heading to the elevators. Angela smiles and greets Mrs. Vazquez first and then wishes Hector good luck before she says,

> "I know that you will be admitted into the Neuro Intensive Care Unit directly after post-operative care.
> I can have your belongings transported there, if you like."

Mrs. Vazquez replies,

> "Oh, thank you.
> That would be great.
> I have most of his belongings in this overnight bag,"

she says as she holds up her husband's bag.

"I only left a few of his items there in his room.
I was going to come back for them later."

The elevator door opens, and Steve dutifully rolls the gurney inside with his patient.

***

Mimi smiles at her granddaughters first before she continues to explain her thoughts,

"You see girls,
there are so many wonderful memories and circumstances that I can personally reflect upon during the entire course of my career.
Nurses have so many, many great happy stories along with the sad, unique and sometimes difficult ones, too."

All at once, Lydia, Ellie and Carla jump up from their seats. They ask the same question in unison,

"But what happens to Hector?
We need to know."

"Ah…, oh, yeah.
I was getting to that.
My nursing assistant and myself packed up the rest of Hector's belongings from his room.
We were especially careful to neatly roll up a poster that he had.
It was a poster of himself running and crossing the finish line while breaking the tape.
It was very clear from the poster that he was very proud of that moment.
Then before the end of our shift, we transported everything ourselves to the ICU.

We saw his entire family nervously waiting for him in the ICU waiting area.

Hector was still in the recovery room.

But the next morning on my coffee break, I went to see him.

His wife and children were all gathered around his bedside as he lay motionless, obviously sedated in his bed.

He was still intubated and on a respirator.

He was actually a very strong man in an average-size body,

but he appeared to be asleep surrounded by huge machines. There were several IV lines exiting from beneath his patient gown's neck and a huge bulky white gauze dressing tightly, but neatly, wrapped around his head.

I looked on from a distance, but I didn't want to interfere with his family praying, so I left."

Mimi clears her throat, then continues,

"Then about two years later, I saw Hector again.

It was at a road race.

I recognized him right away.

He looked exactly how I remembered.

He looked just like he did prior to his surgery.

Actually, he looked just like he did in his poster.

He was an age group winner that day.

I never approached him.

I watched again from a distance,

but I felt a huge sense of satisfaction and relief the very moment I saw him.

It was satisfaction, pride and happiness in just knowing that Hector made a full recovery from cancer and his surgery.

That was the last time I ever saw him."

Mimi smiled as she spoke and remembered.

Chapter Five

A Typical Day, Back in The Day

During the mid 1970s, Bob Julian stands quietly as he leans up against the open doorway of his semi-private hospital room. In complete silence, he watches each nurse emerge quickly from the nurses' station and look into each room as they walk down the long hallway and then toward him. A veteran nursing assistant, Rose, exits from the room next to Bob as she thinks to herself, ***Where did that loud noise come from? I can see that all of the nurses heard it too. They are all wandering around from room to room, searching for the cause of that very loud bang also.*** Bob looks directly into Rose's eyes. He addresses her in a very calm, matter of fact tone and manner as he nods his head in the direction,

"Room 206.

That's where you want to go Rosie."

Rose heeds Bob's warning and quickly makes her way toward Room 206. She runs inside of the room and immediately turns around towards the doorway as she yells out into the hallway,

"Room 206!
We need a crash cart here!
Room 206!"

Rose runs back into the room and calls a code from the patient's phone. Before she even hangs up, she can hear the code being called over the intercom system several times. Before Rose takes another breath, the private room is already filled with her colleagues and the red crash cart. Two of the male medical interns physically scoops Patsy Scott up off from the floor and easily places him down onto the bed. The chief medical resident, Jeff, had already made a quick physical examination of Patsy while he was still lying on the floor as he thinks, *It looks like he pulled the table down with him, breaking the severity of his fall. It most certainly could have been a lot worse. The nurse said the noise was quite loud, crashing is what I heard them describe the noise as. We better get a set of spinal films taken, too.* One nurse had already placed an IV line and drew labs on him, while another nurse had yelled out his vital signs to the crowd. The nurse standing in front of the crash cart primed an IV line and passed it on to the nurse closest to the patient. Jeff asks for Narcan and administers it within a few seconds as his vital signs are being rechecked. The respiratory tech draws blood gases then places an oxygen mask over Patsy's face after checking his oxygen saturation level.

Patsy Scott begins moaning before his eyes eventually open up. He tries to yell out, but only a few guttural sounds emerges from his mouth. He is initially enveloped in complete fear and utter confusion as he sees a dozen or so foggy looking faces looking down on him from above. His eyes react and seem to bulge as he thinks, while trying to grasp at what is possibly happening to him at this very moment, *Shit. What the hell is going on here? Am I dead or something? What are they all doing to me? The last thing I can remember doing is… eating that chocolate candy. Shit, that's it. They must have poisoned me or something. It must have been in that box of candy I got this morning.*

The middle-aged man, slightly rounded around his mid-section coughs up some mucous before he finds his voice,

> "What the hell happened?
> Tell me, what happened to me."

Jeff sighs before he answers his patient,

> "Well, Patsy.
> Did you take something?
> You overdosed on something.
> You overdosed on a narcotic, actually."

The hospital staff slowly begins to exit the room one by one, each expressing relief at the outcome of a successful code. Patsy takes a few deep breaths before he pushes himself up into a sitting position. He partially removes the oxygen mask away from his face before he replies just louder than a whisper,

> "But, but I didn't take anything.
> Honestly, I didn't take anything.
> I must have been poisoned.
> The last thing that I can remember is…"

Patsy pauses and clears his throat again as he looks around his room thinking, *Hey, I have a pretty good crowd going here.* He quickly realizes, *I have their undivided attention,* then he continues to speak to his audience,

> "I remember eating a piece of candy from that box over there,"

He slowly raises his arm up and points towards his small nightstand in the corner of the room, then he quickly adds,

> "I guess I shoulda known better.
> When I came out of the bathroom this morning.
> It was sitting right there on the table neatly wrapped with a bow on it too.
> I thought it was a gift from a friend.
> I love chocolate candy.
> Everyone who knows me, knows how much I love chocolate."

Patsy suddenly stops talking after he hears his own voice and realizes what he just said, *Shit. They found out exactly where I am. This was no accident, that's for sure. It's a message. This is a specific message for me. A message that says, keep your mouth shut fatso, because we know how to find you*. Patsy sighs and stares straight ahead. His skin color is suddenly paled in utter fear. He slowly readjusts the oxygen mask back onto his face and lies completely back against his bed. Patsy's body reacts to his fear by shivering uncontrollably. Jeff instructs his first year medical intern to send the remaining box of candy to the lab for testing. He then looks directly at Patsy's eyes and says,

> "So, sir,
> do you know who would want to hurt or poison you?"

Patsy quickly replies,

> "No, no, no, I misspoke.
> I was very confused.
> I must have taken something all on my own.
> B-b-b-but…, by accident of course.
> Leave that candy here with me.
> There's nothing to be found in there,"

Patsy yells at the intern while in a state of panic. His attempts are successful in gaining his attention. The intern looks up at Patsy before he sets the box of candy back down onto the table. Patsy continues to ramble on,

"I was completely mistaken by the whole thing.
I didn't mean what I said before.
No one would ever try to hurt me.
I don't have any enemies.
Really, I don't,"

Patsy pleads with Jeff and the intern. Then suddenly, all attention is diverted to a loud voice calling out over the loud speaker loudly announcing a code to Room 210 over and over until the entire team finally arrives to Room 210. Jeff and his intern exit Patsy's room and run down the opposite end of the hallway to the destination being announced over the loud speaker. A secondary crash cart arrives to the room at the same moment as Jeff. Jeff looks around the room and diverts his attention to the head nurse on the unit and asks in his usual calm demeanor,

"OK, Donna,
what do we have here?"

Jeff sees a young African American male lying on his back seizing with a padded tongue depressor in his mouth. He listens intently as Donna responds,

"Michael Jones is a new admission to the unit about ten minutes ago from the emergency department.
His diagnosis is, "Grand Mal Seizures."
He does have a history of seizure activity beginning from the age of twelve."

Jeff quickly looks at the emergency room notes and orders written by the emergency room department and makes a request, *"Ten milligrams of Valium IV now,"* as Donna continues to speak. The quick, continuous, violent muscle contractures in Michael's body begin to slow down and finally comes to a halt after the medication is administered. The team looks on while assessing Michael, as a nurse wraps a blood pressure cuff around the patient's upper arm and the respiratory therapist, checks his oxygen saturation level. Donna continues,

> "Michael is an eighteen-year-old male who has been seizure free since age twelve until today.
>
> He has been on a maintenance dose of Dilantin, (medication used to treat Epilepsy), for several years now.
>
> According to his family, he had a seizure at home this morning.
>
> He then had one in the ambulance while en route, and then another one in the emergency room.
>
> Chest x-ray, bloodwork, including Dilantin level and toxicology screen, were drawn, sepsis workup and EKG, all also completed while he was in the emergency room.
>
> His mother reported to the ER nurse, he was recovering from a cold.
>
> He continues to be lethargic since his first episode early this morning."

Angela calls out the patient's vital signs and Jeff nods, acknowledging her response. Janet, one of the nurses standing in front of the crash cart, documents all actual events, vital signs, values, treatments and cares that are rendered before, during and post code onto a form called the *Code Sheet Report,* that is conveniently located on a clipboard attached to each crash cart. Jeff begins to write doctor's orders to be carried out for Michael as he dictates them to Janet, the nursing team leader for the shift. The unit clerk, Elaine, peeks her head inside of the doorway of the now crowded room and searches for Janet and then for nurse Gina. Once she has caught Janet's attention, she says,

> "Hey, Janet, your team is getting a new patient from the ICU into Gina's empty room.
>
> It's Bill; Bill Thomas.
>
> He's back again.

But this time he had surgery for a ruptured spleen.
I told them you were still in a code.
They said they will do the move after lunch.
Is that going to be OK?"

Janet nods her head at Elaine and smiles as she thinks to herself, **OK then. Once we are finished up in here then I'll go and check in on Patsy. Oh, yeah, I have to check with the pharmacy, too. We need to find out when the Factor VIII, (medication used to treat Hemophilia), will be ready for administration for Bob Julien. Then we should be ready for Bill by then. I'm lucky that I have such a great team. We will make it all work because that's what we do.**

Once Jeff is satisfied that Michael is stable, he decides to go back and check in on Patsy. He enters the room and is happy to see Gina is in the process of checking his blood pressure and temperature. He asks Gina,

"Gina, how's his vitals?"

She writes down the results for herself on a small notepad she keeps in her uniform pocket. Gina then tells Jeff her readings before she leaves the room and checks in on her next patient. Rose helps Angela get Michael cleaned up and settled. Angela can see that Michael is still quite lethargic, but he is now responsive and able to answer some questions for her before he falls asleep again. She takes another set of vital signs and checks his IV bottle and IV site and tidies up his room before she feels comfortable enough to leave the room and check in on her other seven patients.

Bill Thomas arrives on the unit after lunch via stretcher, accompanied by his ICU nurse and a hospital transporter. Janet and Jeff are busy administering the Factor VIII to Bob Julien. Gina, Angela and Rose greet Bill and assist in the transfer of Bill from the stretcher onto his bed. Rose immediately grabs a hold of Bill's belongings bag and neatly places it inside of his closet as Gina takes his vital signs. Angela checks his surgical dressing and listens to his lung sounds. Then Gina checks his IV site, right pedal and radial pulses, then continues with her physical assessment of her newest patient. Bill jokes around like always asking,

> "So how's my favorite trio of nurses doing?
> Did you guys miss me?
> I sensed that you were all missing me.
> So, here I am in the flesh."

Rose answers first,

> "Miss you?
> You were here last about a month ago,
> weren't you Bill?
> So, what happened this time?
> How did your spleen rupture?
> Please tell us how this happened."

Bill laughs as he tries to minimize the pain by holding his belly and abdominal dressing with a pillow against them before he answers,

> "That's what I love about you, Rose.
> You tell it like it is, all of the time.
> I always know that you will be honest with me.
> Well, you're right.
> I got into another barfight.
> Barfights are probably the only consistent thing I have going on in my life.
> One of the guys was stomping on me, and he must have ruptured my spleen.
> I don't remember too much of anything else after that."

Angela and Gina listen to Bill's latest bar escapades as they diligently take notes and write down the results of their assessments. Rose looks at Bill with a curious look on her face and asks,

> "But, Bill, did you pick a fight with these guys?

How many of them were there this time?
Were you alone or with the gang?"

> "Yeah, I did kind of pick the fight.
> They were really annoying me.
> Talking garbage, they were.
> So I told them to shut up.
> They ignored me so…
> I caught them by surprise when I removed my prosthetic leg and hit the most annoying fool first with my damn leg.
> You see, I discovered a new use for the damn thing.
> That probably pissed them off.
> Yeah, I think that there was about five of them this time.
> Nah, I was alone.
> My guys weren't there yet.
> I was actually minding my own business having a drink,
> but I think the bartender called the cops once bodies started flying.
> He really saved my butt again.
> And the rest is history."

Then Gina adds,

> "Bill, you are really too much.
> Lucky for you, you can live without a spleen.
> If I remember correctly,
> the last time you were here you got into a barfight and lost your left eye.
> A year ago you got into a fight and lost your left kidney because of that fight.
> It's about two years ago now that you lost your left leg as an outcome of a bar brawl, too.
> Does that all sound right to you, Bill?"

> "That all sounds about right, Gina.
> I'm all right now, heh, heh.
> I still have my left arm, though, heh, heh.
> But to know me is to love me, right ladies?"

Gina, Rose and Angela all laugh as Gina replies,

> "Yeah, that is true, Bill.
> We do love you."

Then a large group of very loud men and women all dressed in black leather enter the private room laughing and joking,

> "Well, well, well,
> look who we have here, fellas.
> We found you, Bill.
> You crazy son of a B --
> Oh, hello ladies.
> Excuse my French,"

says Johnny, a very large, but tall man covered in various forms of tattoos, easily seen from his neck down. He wore a sleeveless black leather jacket branding their club emblem across the back of it. It was a fairly obvious assumption to the entire nursing staff that Johnny held a position of high authority within the club members. He reeked of self-confidence through his very rough exterior, as he gracefully glides across the room over toward Bill to give him a fist bump, followed by a huge bearhug. Angela and Rose nonchalantly look on at the club greeting as they quietly leave the room. Gina follows them out into the hallway after she addresses her patient, while speaking above the loud chatter in the room,

> "Bill, we will leave you with your visitors for now,
>   but I'll be back later.
> Now behave yourself,"

Gina smiles at Bill on her way out of the door. Bill smiles back as he thinks to himself, *Oh, but I always do behave myself, in the hospital that is. Well sort of, anyway. You guys have always taken really good care of me, I must admit.*

***

The girls look at each other and then at their great grandmother awaiting for her to continue with her story. Ellie says,

"I have to go home, but I can't leave until you tell us what happened to Patsy, Michael, Bill and Bob."

Angela recognizes she has their full attention and continues,

"Well, sadly.

Michael had another seizure that night in the intensive care unit and then passed away.

The entire staff was very upset about Michael.

We heard a few months later that Michael's autopsy revealed a malignant stage IV brain tumor as the cause of his death.

Patsy was discharged a few days later.

The rumor after his discharge was that he entered some type of witness protection program after that.

Bill stayed in the hospital for about another week or so,

and about a year later he and his gang all moved south.

I think South Jersey is what I heard, and we never saw them again after that.

Bob came back every so often for his Factor VIII treatment,

but I only remember seeing him for maybe eight more years after that.

Then I don't know whatever happened to him.

I heard that he was the oldest living Hemophiliac living along the east coast, at that time.

He was a funny guy.

A nice guy and very funny, too.

I remember he was always telling us jokes.

Thinking back, I think he enjoyed making us all laugh.

Back then we worked very hard every day, but we had fun doing it, too."

Chapter Six

Working Pediatrics

Her very lean, tiny, timid body looks even smaller as she sits up tall but quietly on top of the over-sized looking emergency department gurney. If not for her yellow wavy sun kissed hair, she is barely noticeable, hopelessly lost within several thin layers of plain white sheets and blankets. She ponders nervously to herself, *I wonder, what is going to happen to me now? Maybe, I shouldn't have told them the whole entire truth. Maybe, I should have said it was all an accident. Yeah, I wonder if I tell them that I meant to say it was an accident, would they believe me? I can say that I was nervous and that… Who am I kidding, I messed up. What are they going to do to me and my mommy now? I'm so very scared right now.* She shivers uncontrollably because of all of the thoughts that keep flooding her mind as her heart beats rapidly, mostly out of fear. It is the fear of uncertainty that is sure to show up again too soon. All that Melissa knows right now is, *I have to stay here in the hospital for a few more days. That is what they told me.* A child well beyond her six years of life is learning how to hone in on her survival instincts unlike most of her classmates at school. The two nurses transporting her to the pediatric unit spent the last few hours telling her very traditional and made up fairytales, trying desperately to divert her attention from the ugly truth of her present-day life. Pediatric floor nurse, Carolyn, greets Melissa inside of her hospital room as she carefully helps transport her from the cold emergency room gurney onto her cozy warm hospital bed. She places the nurse call bell button very close to Melissa, pins it to the sheet beside her pillow and instructs her,

"Now, do not get out of bed by yourself.

If you need any help at all,
press this little red button right here.

It may take a few minutes, but either I or one of my helpers will come in as soon as we possibly can to help you.

Now get some rest.

Do you feel any discomfort in your feet right now Melissa?"

Carolyn asks as she examines Melissa's gauze dressings covering both of her feet before she covers her up with a light rainbow colored blanket. She then records Melissa's vital signs onto her worksheet before leaving the room. Carolyn had received report earlier on Melissa, her new admission over the telephone, before she actually arrived up on the unit. She feels an overwhelming heaviness in her heart as she thinks, *How could someone, a mother at that, do this to their own child, nevertheless any child? I can't believe that she was so angry at her and felt she needed to teach her daughter a lesson. A lesson she will never forget. Oh my God, she filled the bathtub up with scalding hot water.* Carolyn shudders at the thought because she still cannot believe a mother can purposely do this awful, awful thing to her own child. *Then she picks Melissa's petite little body up into the air and dips her toes in. She dips her toes on purpose into this scalding hot water, leaving her with third degree burns. How could she do that? It's a good thing her neighbor called the police on her when she heard Melissa screaming uncontrollably. I can't even imagine what this poor child has been through at the hands of her very own mother. This is obviously not the first time she has abused her. Poor, poor baby. Hmm, her chart says that social services is already on the case. This little girl is already scarred physically, and I am sure mentally for life. Well, I better start on her admission paperwork. It won't get done on its own, and I certainly don't want to stay late doing it.* This scenario haunts the entire staff for many more years.

As Carolyn leaves Melissa's room she can hear the unit's

resident baby boy, Brian, crying. Nurse Nina walks toward Carolyn and says,

> "Go, girl, I got it.
> Do your admission.
> You don't want to be here late doing it.
> Besides, we have another admission coming soon.
> It will be my time with Bri-Bri today."

> "Thanks, Nina,"

Carolyn says as she heads toward the nurses' station to do her charting. Nina makes her way down the darkened hallway to Brian's room as she thinks, *I can't believe Brian has been here with us for a year already. When they do find placement for him, we are all going to miss him. Of course he doesn't understand what is happening, but he was really happy and excited over the birthday party we made for him. We are all basically his family, we have raised him this far. It is really hard to place a baby somewhere who already has so many medical issues.* She walks into the room and sees Brian lying on his stomach crying,

> "Awe, Bri-Bri.
> What's wrong baby boy?
> OK, let's change your diaper first.
> Then how about a bottle after that?
> Does that sound good to you?"

Brian's eyes light up the moment he sees the familiar friendly face enter his room. He begins to coo immediately, satisfied he is no longer alone inside of his room. Nina washes her hands before she dons her exam gloves. She changes his soiled diaper as she hums a nursery rhyme song softly to him, *Hush little baby, don't you cry…*

As she continues humming, Nina makes herself comfortable in the large wooden rocking chair located in the far corner of Brian's private room. She places the nipple portion of the plastic bottle inside of Brian's mouth. She swirls the bottle around awaiting for Brian to latch onto the nipple as she thinks, *Poor baby. You still struggle with feeding. Your mama did you no justice, taking all of those drugs while she was pregnant with you. It's outrageous to learn that she purposely gets pregnant because it makes it easier for her to find a vein to shoot up her drugs into. I know that I shouldn't judge anyone, but it's a horrific reason to have a baby that she doesn't intend to keep anyway.* She sighs as she recognizes Brian is becoming frustrated and irritated as he struggles with the nipple from the plastic baby bottle. Nina swirls the nipple around in his mouth again and again until he is finally successful, as she hums the soothing song over and over again. *My goodness, Bri. I wonder if you will ever meet your siblings. They are also in the social service system as well. I think that there is five or six of you all together now, unless your mama is pregnant again, of course. Hmmm, Hush little baby, hmmm, hmmm.* Nina slowly rocks Brian until he finally falls asleep inside of her arms. *Poor sweet Brian. I pray things get better for you. You are the most innocent of innocent born into drug addiction. A choice given to you, not made by you. I remember you had to be weaned off of whatever you were born addicted to. I can already see the effects of it on you. A year old and you can't sit up on your own yet. Heck, you just began to pick your head up and roll over successfully. I am sure that there will be some mental delay to go along with the physical, but while you are here with us now, we are your family now, and we love you, sweet little Bri.* Nina places the almost empty bottle down on top of the nightstand, and with Brian in her arms, she slowly inches her way over to the crib and eases Brian down onto the mattress without waking him. She purposely places him on his side, propped up by a foam slanted pillow made and used specifically for the purpose of propping him onto his side.

Nina quietly tiptoes into the next room to check in on one of her other patients, *Oh good. She's asleep*, Nina thinks as she whispers to the mother of her patient,

"Are you alright?

Do you need me to do anything or get you anything for you?

Would you like a few extra blankets or towels?"

The mom lovingly peers at her sleeping baby inside of the crib, then directly over at her husband snoring ever so lightly on a sleeper chair before she whispers back,

"No, we are fine for now.
Thank you, Nina.
She actually had a few more little seizures.
Carolyn was at the desk and she came in.
She already spoke with our pediatrician."

Then she wipes away a single tear that escapes from the wells of her eyes. Her heart aches as she stares at her eight-month-old petite little baby girl with physical characteristics of a four-week-old infant. She wants to soak up every single moment possible that she has left with her. Debbie smiles at her tiny daughter as she pulls her chair up as close as she possibly can to the crib and lays her upper body next to her baby. She coddles little Clara and whispers sweet secrets into her ear, *I know that you can hear me despite what everyone says. Mommy and daddy love you so very, very much. You are and will always be our sweet little blessing, Clara.* Debbie tries hard not to cry, but the tears flow anyway. Debbie sees something that briefly warms her heart, but this small act lasts a lifetime, ***I am sure that was just a smile. Clara smiled at me. She is telling me that she loves us too. I am sure of it.***

Nina backs out of the room slowly and quietly as she ponders, ***Anencephaly. So very sad. The seizures are getting worse, too. She basically has so very little brain function within her tiny underdeveloped brain. Poor mom has had to feed her through a feeding tube her whole very young life. They say it is only a matter of time now. There is no cure. Who knows why her brain never grew. Who knows why she has lived this long. The specialist did not expect her to live a day after she was born, but she did. Debbie knew during her pregnancy that her baby had a defect, but she couldn't*** *bring herself to terminate the pregnancy as recommended by her physicians. I wonder if they will have another baby later on down the road. Right now Clara is everything to them. She is their whole life. I would probably feel the same way, if given the same circumstance, I think.*

Carolyn waves to Nina when she sees her approaching the nurses' station, obviously deep in thought. When she reaches the desk, Carolyn asks,

"Lois needs a hand turning her patient in the PICU, (Pediatric Intensive Care Unit).

Do you want to go in and help her?

I don't mind going, if you want to take a break before the new admission arrives.

I am almost done with my paperwork.

Actually, the new admission coming up is for the PICU.

We will have to help Lois anyway with the admission assessment and paperwork.

She is a direct admission from the recovery room."

Nina curls her nose in thought for a quick second and replies,

"Carolyn, you finish up your admission for Melissa, and I'll go and help Lois.

She has the little boy who was the drowning victim from yesterday, right?"

"Yeah,

that's right.

He is the eight-year-old boy who fell into the family pool through the pool cover.

I think that he was tangled up in the cover.

By the time they realized where he was, he had to have been in there about twenty minutes or so.

They were able to revive him, but the second EEG done a little while ago was flat.

He is legally brain dead.
The neurologist is speaking with the family now.
Lois wants to make sure he is cleaned up and presentable before they come back to the unit."

"OK, then.
Let me go in there now,"

Nina replies as she walks into the PICU, located across from the nurses' station.

'Lois, I'll help you."

"OK, thanks, Nina.
His parents should be back soon.
I want to make sure he looks good for his family when they return.
Right now they are in conference with the neurologist."

Nina dons a pair of gloves after she applies a protective yellow gown. She looks sadly at the young boy, Josh, lost amongst all of the hospital equipment needed to sustain life. His controlled rhythmic breathing pattern is now regulated by a machine, a ventilator, rather than his own body. She cannot help but to notice how distorted his facial features and general appearance is due to the advanced swelling, and her sadness is just so overwhelming, ***Oh no. This is so very tragic. I cannot imagine what his family is going through right now.*** As Nina and Lois place the top sheet over Josh's torso, they can hear wails of grief approaching from a distance. The immediate family gather closely together inside the waiting area first, attempting to regain some type of composure. After a few moments, they notify Lois that they have decided to act as recommended by the neurologist. Josh's dad, Mr. Palumbo, approaches Lois and says,

"We have decided to sign the papers.
Can you tell Dr. Chin for us?"

Then Mr. Palumbo weeps uncontrollably into his own hands, covering his entire face, *I cannot believe my Josh is gone. My baby boy is no longer with us, the doctor said. Why weren't we stricter with him? How could this happen to my boy? God, please take me instead, please.* Lois tries to console him, but she knows that whatever she says will never bring him comfort or peace. *He is obviously filled with grief and guilt as he blames himself for not protecting his son. It is not his fault.* The Palumbo family gather around Josh. Each grieving member expresses their love to him in their own unique way. Mrs. Palumbo is completely beside herself as she whispers into Josh's ear, *We love you baby boy, so very, very much. I am so sorry that I wasn't there for you when you needed me. God, please forgive me.*

The neurologist, Dr. Chin, eventually arrives to the unit, accompanied by his pediatric resident, a respiratory technician, and the hospital priest to administer last rights. The resident extubates Josh by removing the tube from his mouth that is connected to the mechanical machine responsible for the artificial breathing. Josh never moved during and after becoming free from the respirator. Without oxygen, his heart ceases to beat, and he is pronounced dead. Lost and heartbroken, the Palumbo family sits in vigil around Josh.

Heather Daniels is wheeled up by two recovery room nurses into Room 2 inside of the PICU via her hospital bed. Pediatric nurses, Lois and Carolyn, help her get settled into her new room after checking her vital signs. Lois does her physical assessment of her new patient, including an assessment of her newly abdominal surgical dressing and IV site. Heather is assigned a sitter by administration for suicide watch until she is officially cleared by psychiatry. Lois instinctively circles a small circle around the bloody drainage in pen on Heather's abdominal wound dressing (as an indicator of increased bleeding beneath the dressing if the drainage exceeds the pen mark). She likes to think to herself while she assesses her patients, *OK, Heather is a fifteen-year-old white, lean, healthy female. She is status post self-inflicted GSW, (gunshot wound) to the abdomen. She is presently lethargic but easily arousable, oriented to person, place and time when asked. Her pupils are equal and reactive to light. Abdominal dressing is dry and intact with a small amount of bloody drainage noted and circled. She has decreased bowel sounds present X4 quadrants. IV site, 18-Guage to the right fore-arm is healthy with a liter of D5RL patent at 75cc/hour via pump, 975cc LIB (left in bag). Positive pulses are strong to all four ex-tremities, MAE (moving all extremities). Lung sounds are equal and clear bilaterally. Denies pain or discomfort at present. Her sitter is at the bedside. Ah… assessment is done, now all I have to do is all of the admission paperwork.*

Carolyn checks in on the Palumbo family and offers her heartfelt condolences. They are all clearly distressed but have decided at is time to depart for home. She feels the heaviness in her soul watching the backs of Josh Palumbo's family walk away slowly toward the exit sign. Their heads are bowed down in grief, arms wrapped tightly around each other while tears and sobs flow freely from each member.

***

Melissa's external wounds eventually heal and she makes a full recovery. Her introduction into the world of social ser-vices is really not so unique. Sadly, too many young children are lost within the overcrowded system. Melissa was no different. She does get placed with a family member until she is eventu-ally returned to her mother. Brian eventually gets placed into a foster home in another jurisdiction. We really don't know anything more about Brian's whereabouts except that he does eventually test positive for the HIV virus. Baby Clara went into respiratory distress and died the next morning in her parents' arms. Heather recovered from her self-inflicted wound. It was determined by psychiatry that it was not a suicide attempt. Her intention was to hide and dispose of a fetus that she believed was growing inside of her. She feared she would be disciplined if her secret was exposed. Her misguided plan was not well thought out. Although she may have missed a month of her menstruation, it was not due to pregnancy but because of an ovarian cyst. The bullet missed her major organs except for one, her uterus, requiring her to have a hysterectomy during the abdominal repair. It was later recommended she enter an adolescent psychiatric facility for counseling.

Regardless of the unit, department or facility where you hang your coat or have a locker in, each shift, day or week, is unique in its own nature. In the medical field, we never know who or what circumstance is entering through our doorway. With growing experience, we learn to acclimate, readjust and improvise each and every scenario to the very best positive outcome we possibly can. For most, we hurt and cry along with our patients. As medical professionals we grow as we learn, but we are humans first.

Chapter Seven

We Welcome All and Care For All, Regardless

She and her colleagues, full-time float nurses, receive their assignments each day from the Nursing Administration Office according to the needs of each unit. Upon receiving their assignments, Angela and Marina walk toward the emergency department together. Angela looks around as they make their way through the seemingly endless hall filled with potential patients on gurneys leading up to the main nursing desk, or the hub of it all, and is briefly lost in thought, *Oh my. It looks like it is going to be another very busy day here. There seems to be people in almost every possible open space and cubbyhole. What is going on*? Joanne, the charge nurse, smiles as she tells them her plans for the entire shift.

"Hello, ladies, and welcome.

I am happy to see you both again.

Marina, you are going to be working in the overflow holding area upfront.

Everyone there has a bed upstairs, but they aren't ready yet.

Once you are able to get them to the floors, I have

some people here in the long hall and on the strip that I will send up to you.

Angela, I need you here on the strip, (An area containing six fully equipped exam rooms along the opposite long hallway).

It's busy, as you can see.

I have a nurse, Janice, coming in.

She'll be here in about four hours.

When she gets here, she'll take the strip from you.

Then, I need you to go and help Marina in holding."

Angela immediately takes report from the off going nurse on the patients in her six exam rooms. Helen talks quickly and introduces Angela to the occupants in each room as they stroll down the hall,

"In Room 1, we have Jack S. here.

He is a thirty-year-old male who has *"accidentally"* swallowed a foreign object again, whole.

X-ray confirms he swallowed a toothbrush, whole.

It is lodged somewhere within his esophagus.

You should take a look at the films when you have a chance.

It is quite interesting.

He does have a history of swallowing foreign objects in the past,

but this is his largest piece so far.

I suppose he has been working his way up to it.

He is presently NPO, (nothing by mouth).

IV fluids RL infusing into his left forearm at 75ml/hour.

He is on call and prepped for endoscopy, EGD, (Esophagogastroduodenoscopy) and removal of a foreign object.

His consent is signed and witnessed, and his chart is in order.

So he is all ready to go when endo calls for him.
Oh, psych was already here to see him."

Helen knocks on his door and introduces Angela as his oncoming nurse before they move on to Room 2.

"Room 2 is Serena L.
She is a twenty-five-year-old female who presents with stage four malignant ovarian cancer.
She is awaiting for her assigned bed up on the oncology unit to become available.
Housekeeping is in the process of cleaning her room now.
I already gave her report to the oncology nurse.
Serena is status/post postpartum six months for a baby girl, she is para two, gravida two, (two pregnancies/two living children).
Sadly, her malignancy was discovered during her pregnancy.
She began her chemo regimen post-delivery and round three was administered yesterday in the outpatient clinic.
Today she developed a high fever of 103F, nausea and projectile vomiting.
She is NPO with a nasogastric tube connected to low intermittent suction draining copious amounts of green bilious content.
IVF D5RL patent at 125ml/hour.
She does have malignant ascites, (fluid buildup in abdomen).
Can you measure her abdominal girth for me?
I just medicated her for pain and meant to get her girth then, but I became distracted and busy."

Angela nods her head in agreement as she accepts the measuring tape from Helen and records info onto her clipboard for later reference. Then she peeks in on Serena as she sleeps, before they walk toward the next room.

"Room 3 is -- you know the nurses' assistant Lizzie who works in our psych unit, right?" Angela nods yes in disbelief.

She's here in Room 3.

They brought her in after she was attacked by a female patient on their ward.

The patient lured her into her bedroom and bit a huge chunk out of Lizzie's arm.

Then, the patient who weighs over three hundred pounds, she then plopped herself down in front of the closed door, preventing the staff members from entering the room for almost an hour.

Plastics (Plastic Surgery Surgeon), was here already.

She was administered a dose of Tetanus.

Her wound was cleaned and sutured by Plastics.

She was just administered pain meds and started on IV antibiotics.

She actually has a bed upstairs, but it won't be ready for another hour.

I already gave report on her also.

You just have to transfer her up when her bed is ready."

Helen hands Angela the charts for the three patients she just spoke of and then they move on.

"Room 4 is Anthony J.

A twenty-four-year old male in Sickle Cell Crisis.

IVF is running at 150ml/hour via central line inserted into his left subclavian.

X-ray already confirmed placement.

I just administered his IV pain med.

After pain management sees him, they are considering on initiating a drip for him to relieve his pain.

Transport is picking up blood from the lab, and then

they will transfer him up to the floor for you.
His bed upstairs is ready."

Angela peeks her head inside of the room to greet Anthony. He looks at her and smiles back right away before he says,

"Oh, hey.
It is so good seeing you again.
I will be going upstairs soon.
Please come up and visit me."

Angela smiles at him as she thinks back, *My goodness, we have known each other for a very long time now. I remember the young boy I first met many years ago in Sickle Cell Crisis, must be ten years now. Hmm, great kid who was handed a very raw deal, but at least he has a great supportive family.*

"Oh, yes, Anthony.
I will definitely come and see you upstairs later on.
Oh, look, Simon is here now to take you upstairs to your room.
See you up there later, kid."

Simon greets Angela and Helen first as Helen hands him Anthony's chart before he enters Room 4. Angela can hear Simon greet Anthony before he slowly guides the gurney out of the exam room and towards the elevator. Helen and Angela walk toward the next room and Helen continues with her report,

"OK, in Room 5 we have Stanley B.
Stanley had been fishing today.
He came into the department with a hook lodged into the right side of his face, his cheek to be exact.
I know nothing about fishing, so I'm not really sure how this happened.
The team is in there now with him, removing the hook.
He'll be discharged home when they are all done

with him.”

She shuffles the charts around in her arms then continues,

> “OK now.
> In Room 6, we have Cinthia D.
> Cinthia is a fifty-five-year-old female who presents to the department with high fever, chills, extreme fatigue and weight loss that has progressed on and off for several months now.
> She recently has developed a wet cough.
> Her chest x-ray shows a left lower lobe infiltrate, but it is suspicious.
> She is actually having a Cat Scan as we speak.
> We have her under respiratory and airborne precautions for now.
> We did a full sepsis and HIV workup; sputum specimen was sent to the lab as well.
> During her H&P (history & physical), she reported to have had unprotected sex once about a year ago with a gentlemen she met at a bar.
> She had been going through a very difficult divorce and met someone one night when she went out with her friends.
> We started her on IV Bactrim.
> I feel bad for her; she’s really nice.
> Well, that’s all I have for you.
> I’ll clean up Anthony’s room for you so you can call your next patient in from the waiting room.
> As quickly as we call people inside, it seems like ten more people walk into the waiting area.
> Have a great shift, girl.”

Angela drops off her charts of all her patients at the desk. She is just in time to see two familiar EMS workers wheel in a gurney with a young woman propped up into a high fowlers position with an oxygen mask covering her face and she thinks,

Her color is just awful, and she is definitely struggling to breathe.
Now curious, she listens to the report from EMS being given to
Joanne and the emergency department attending, Dr. Max Taylor.

> "We have twenty-nine-year-old Gloria Moreno.
>
> Slightly obese but generally in good health, was reported by her spouse.
>
> Her husband states that last night she developed a high fever, chills, headache, dizziness and light-headedness.
>
> This morning she developed some confusion, rapid breathing and a rash.
>
> He thought it was all related to the fever, but her mother who lives with them called EMS.
>
> She began to de-sat (decrease in oxygen saturation level), in the bus, so we placed a mask on her.
>
> She has two 18-guage IV's in each arm.
>
> Oh, and the mother said that she is menstruating for a few days now, and that she has been run down."

Max wrinkles his forehead as he quickly takes a closer look at
Gloria and listens to the report being given by Billy and Marianna from EMS. He immediately blurts out some orders to his
team,

> "OK people, let's get respiratory in here now and place her on a ventilator.
>
> We need blood gases, sepsis workup, and a full set of cultures done STAT (Immediately).
>
> Let's get a foley catheter into her, and we need to do a pelvic exam while we are at it.
>
> Sally, please call for an ID (Infectious Disease) consult.
>
> Looks like _Toxic Shock Syndrome_ to me, people."

As he spoke, she was already being wheeled into an area out

of the hallway and into an empty room. Everyone quickly responds to every order given, and within minutes all orders were completed. After the pelvic exam, an old looking tampon was removed from Gloria, and now Max felt confident his diagnosis was accurate. Once all of her cultures were obtained; blood, urine, throat, nasal, vaginal and rectal, they were carefully labeled and sent to the lab. A spinal tap was performed before she was started on IV antibiotics as recommended by ID. A bed soon became available, and Gloria was immediately admitted to the ICU, (Intensive Care Unit).

Janice arrives to work early, and Angela is anxious to be relieved from her assigned area along the strip. ***Hopefully the rest of the shift will be a little less hectic in overflow with Marina***, thinks Angela while she walks toward overflow. Marina and Angela team up and are able to commit to a steady consistent workflow where Marina completes the needed paperwork and gives report on the patients to their assigned units. Angela then prepares the patients physically and emotionally before she transports them to the floors. As the patients leave the overflow area, their areas are quickly cleaned and replaced with patients awaiting admission to the floors coming from the long hall and the strip. Marina finishes up the paperwork she had been working on when she catches a glimpse of Angela returning to the station pushing an empty gurney in front of her and smiles, ***Ah, teamwork. We make a great working team together,*** is all that she can think of.

***

Angela sits back in her seat and smiles at her granddaughters. Her mind wanders, ***WOW. I remember that day well and so many more just like that, as if it were yesterday. We worked very well together as a team. Actually, for the most part, everyone I worked with back then were great. Now let's see. Oh, yes, Jack S had*** *his toothbrush removed. I actually knew him from middle school. We were friends but lost track of each other after that. I am not sure if he remembered me, but I would say he had a great deal of issues that needed to be resolved. I never saw him again after that day, so I don't know whatever became of him.*

Serena L. from Room 2 sadly lived in a great deal of pain for two more weeks. I did visit her up on the oncology unit several times. I wasn't working the day she passed away, but it was heartbreaking to watch her suffer. I heard that her husband eventually remarried. Lizzie from Room 3, healed well and eventually returned to work. I did see Anthony J. up on the unit later that night as I had promised. He was in and out of the hospital in Sickle Cell Crisis for the next ten years. Whenever Anthony was admitted into the hospital, myself and a great many of my colleagues made it our business to visit him. He sort of became a part of our extended family. He eventually passed away from complications of his disease. Stanley B. was discharged after his fishing hook was removed from his face. I heard that he took the hook home with him as a reminder to be more cautious when casting his line, or possibly just as a souvenir.

Angela sighs long and hard, then continues while deep in thought, *Hmm, Cinthia D... She was admitted into the hospital and eventually was given a positive diagnosis of HIV. She was started on a treatment plan and then discharged home when her IV antibiotics were completed. I don't remember ever seeing her again. Gloria Moreno, now that was a very sad case. She ended up with many complications that left her in a vegetative state. After a year in the hospital, she ended up being placed into a long-term care facility. I never saw Gloria again after she was discharged from the hospital, but I heard that many years later her family passed away in a terrible accident. Sadly, she outlived her entire family and passed away a year after they did.*

Chapter Eight

All Work, Some Play,
Many Tears

The medical field is made up of an entirely different sort of breed. We have our own language used to describe, prescribe, diagnose and communicate amongst each other. Our work schedules include all holidays and most weekends because our place of employment doesn't close and is open for business 24/7. Most of us have missed and will miss too many important family gatherings with a heavy heart and not because we want to, but because we have to. When our work shift is over, it's not over and our non-medical partners and spouses usually don't get it. You see, we want to sprint out of the door the moment our shift is over, but we can't. It is our duty to stay until we give up our report to the oncoming shift, finish our assignments and complete our charting or documentation for all of our patients. "Because if it is not charted, it wasn't done," is the motto we are taught as nurses. If your relief does not show, then you wait and continue working until one does show up.

Although our shifts are long and our work is exhausting, we are human, too. So we cry when we hurt, some of us even become cranky when we are tired and are not completely infallible as we may appear to be, all because we are human. We thrive to give excellent, compassionate, and accurate care to each and every one of our patients, but are now encouraged that good customer service with a smile is our major priority because healthcare has become a business. Regardless, most of us are human first, loaded with various emotions and some quirks just as everyone else.

***

The sun's rays seem to focus on the softball field this spring day as if it were a warm summer afternoon. Nurses hurriedly gave their off-going report to the oncoming shift, then quickly changed into clothes they brought in that morning. Eight-hour shifts were still implemented during this time, the early `80s, but talks were in the works to offer the now popular twelves. The girls arrive at the field awaiting their opponents, nurses against the female interns and residents. A few male nurses and attendings also arrive for support and to take on the role as umpires. Dr. Frank stood by first base as he watched the pitcher, Dr. Lisa, throw her first pitch to nurse Kat. The nurses in the dugout all sigh in unison as the ball swiftly lands in the catcher's mitt and Dr. Jeff yells out, *Strike One*. The nurses in and out of the dugout think, ***Damn. Dr. Lisa is really serious. We just wanted to have a friendly game. She actually looks good pitching, and she plays as if she played on a team... Hmm, maybe high school and college.***

The interns and residents won that game, but the nurses gave them a run for their money that afternoon. It was the first of many games played throughout the years. It served as a source of fun amongst colleagues who respect and work with each other under very stressful situations on a daily basis. The other stress reliever for some was the ever famous *liver rounds* held on an occasional Friday night at a local bar hosted by the Attending Physicians.

***

Blaring lights can be seen from afar while the distinct sound from the siren is heard from a distance as the ambulance backs into the ambulance bay of the local hospital. Two paramedics carefully wheel out the gurney from the rear of the bus, also accompanied by Burn Unit Physician and Director, Dr. Gil Hodges, as his burn unit team awaits the arrival of their newest patient. She is suddenly whisked away into the designated elevator and up into the sterile unit specifically equipped and intentionally designed for the purpose of caring and treating severe burns. The young high school student, Lila Johnson, was found by firefighters in her bed, as her home was almost completely engulfed in flames. She was not expected to survive her injuries when she was found and was vicariously rushed to a smaller hospital close by the fire for immediate care while rescuers attend to her. The emergency room attending immediately notifies Dr. Hodges, Burn Centre Director from the closest Level I Trauma Hospital with its brand new state of the art, fifteen private room burn unit located about thirty miles away,

"Hello, Gil? Gil Hodges?
This is Ira Jacobs, ED attending from Doctors.
I just received a patient in our ED, but we are not equipped to care for her.
As you already know, we don't have a burn unit here.
She suffers from smoke inhalation and third degree burns to about seventy percent of her body.
It doesn't look good for her,
but she's only sixteen..."

Dr. Hodges listens intently into his cellphone and suddenly blurts out,

> "Say no more, Ira.
> I actually live close by to you.
> I just got home, but…
> I'm on my way there now.
> I'll help you stabilize her, and then we'll transfer her to my unit."

The complete team is ready for Lila as she is rolled into Dr. Hodges' unit, or as some of his colleagues has described it as, *Gil's new Baby*. The nurses have already prepared intravenous anesthetics and pain medication. Her vital signs are taken and intravenous lines checked for patency. An intrajugular triple lumen central line had been placed at the previous hospital with three lines of various IV medication mixed with IV fluid infusing through her lines. Her room has been meticulously sterilized and prepared for her arrival. She is wheeled into the tank room first after her medications are administered and her endotracheal tube (breathing tube placed orally for purpose of intubation), is connected to a respirator. Dr. Hodges had previously instructed his team on the plan of care for Lila while en route to the hospital. He knew that his team would have everything readily prepared prior to her arrival. Lila feels as though she is watching everything being done to and for her from a few feet away, *Is that me they are working on? If it is, I don't recognize her. Her skin is gone! Oh my God, what happened to me? All I remember is mommy and Joe fighting. She told him that she had had enough and she wants him out of her house, and then I went to bed. The next thing I can remember is coughing in my sleep, a lot of smoke everywhere, and then someone saying, she's still alive. And now here I am, but where is, "here?" Oh, they are talking again. Let me listen to them. Maybe I'll get some answers to my questions. Oh, it looks like they are hosing me down on this metal bed or something. I look like I am in a great deal of pain but asleep at the very same time. How is this all possible? This must be all a movie or a very bad dream, I hope.*

Dr. Hodges, his partner, and first assistant quickly cut away at some of the dead and damaged tissue (debridement), then methodically place medicated dressings over the affected areas. A specific area is treated at this time, then she is immediately taken to her new hospital room and bed, *Room #4,* directly adjacent to the oval nurses' station. The plexiglass walled room makes observation easily obtainable to the nursing staff, and her vital signs are easily monitored through her cardiac monitor accessible at the nurses' station as well. Dr. Hodges instructs the team during rounds,

"We can tank another portion of her body tomorrow.

I don't think she can handle much more than that at one time.

Her wounds are so severe, let's just hope she will make it through the week.

It is a great deal of stress on her heart.

And basically because of the degree, amount, and severity of her wounds, the risk of infection, sepsis and major organ failure is overwhelming.

Continue with the antibiotic treatment, pressors and pain management as I have ordered.

Also, keep a close watch on her vital signs, intake and outputs, too.

Call me if there are any changes in her condition.

Dr. Kim, let's see if we can get another line into her.

I need to get a little sleep.

I have a skin graft at one this afternoon on Mrs. Bell.

I'll be in my *on call room* if you need me."

Nurse Karina arrives to work early as usual, *I really hate surprises. This is why I like to make my own rounds first on my patients before taking report,* she thinks to herself as she peaks her head into Lila's room. ***Oh my. What happened to you? Hmm, it says here that your name is Lila Johnson on your Kardex, but honestly you are so badly burned...*** a tear suddenly escapes from Karina's eyes as she continues with her thoughts... ***That just by looking at you, I can't distinguish your sex, age or even skin color for that matter! My God, how have you survived thus far? And the pain you must be in, I cannot even imagine.*** Anna, the night nurse, catches a glimpse of Karina in front of Room 4. She motions for her to come and sit by her in front of the nurses' station cardiac monitor display, (one large monitor equipped to display cardiac rhythms, vital signs, and more for each patient on the unit). Karina looks at Anna before she sits next to her and instinctively prints out rhythms for her two assigned patients required for documentation. Anna says,

> "Let me give you bed #4's report out here in the nurses' station, and then we can walk in her room for our round report.
> We assigned you only two patients this morning because she has a lot going on.
> Your second patient will be a transfer up to the floors when they have a bed available for her.
> As of now, she doesn't have a bed yet.
> You had her the other day, so you know her.
> I just did her dressing change for you, too.
> All you have is her vitals, meds, and report if she gets a bed on one of the surgical units.
> Eileen is in charge this morning.
> She'll help you."

Karina nods her head in agreement and replies,

> "OK.
> Do we have a nurse's aide coming in today, I hope?"

> "Oh, yeah.
> We called Regina in, even though it is her day off.

> She'll be in before ten.
> So you are on your own until she can get here.
> After I give you report, I can help you turn and position Lila, if you like.
> I don't mind,"

Anna replies to Karina, then starts her report.

Once Anna finishes up on her verbal report, both nurses wash their hands, then apply masks, gown and glove up before entering Room #4. Karina looks around the dimly lit room before turning on the overhead lights. She quickly takes a look at the respirator settings, **OK. This looks right.** Then she checks the IV fluids for correct fluid and rate of flow on the IV pumps. She is relieved knowing that Anna just hung all fresh bags an hour ago. **Oh, good. My IVs will be good for most of my shift.** She then checks the cardiac monitor and takes a new set of readings, quickly assesses Lila's central line dressing, and notices the dressing is dated for today. Anna had mentioned during report that she changed all of her IV tubing and central line dressings. With a nurse on each side of the bed, they carefully turn and reposition Lila as they continue to talk in a whisper. Karina winces as if she were the one being moved and turned while thinking to herself, **She must be in a horrendous amount of pain. Poor baby**. Then she says to Anna while assessing her patient's skin,

> "I hope she pulls through all of this, Anna.
> If she does, it will be a very long recovery.
> So, you said she was asleep when the fire broke out?"

Anna nods her head as she points out several areas of Lila's body that concerns her before she answers Karina,

> "Yes, I also saw the story on the news.
> It was on several news stations.
> Didn't you see it?"

Anna sighs, then continues,

"Yes, the firemen rescued Lila from her bed.

The news report said that there were two more bodies found at the scene.

A man and a woman, both deceased.

They think that it was a murder-suicide.

They seem to think that the man killed the woman, set the house on fire, and then killed himself.

So sad.

I don't understand why things like this happens.

It's all so very senseless.

I understand that Lila has an aunt who lives in Georgia.

She is her mother's sister who will be flying in this week.

She is her next of kin."

Karina looks at Lila and thinks, *Oh my, poor baby. How terrible and heartbreaking this whole story is*. Her heart feels so heavy with sadness and grief for Lila and for the very, very long and painful road of recovery ahead of her; that is, if she does survive.

Lila looks down at her own severely deformed looking body and then at the two nurses caring for her. She struggles to hear their whispers over the machine breathing for her in a concise but even rhythm, and she thinks as she listens to the words spoken, *No-o-o-o… it can't be true; my mommy is dead. She is gone forever, and Joe killed her. I guess he meant it all those times he said, I'll never let you leave me. I'd rather see you dead first. We never believed he was serious about that. We thought that it was just his usual rantings. Oh my God, he killed my mommy, and he tried to kill me, too.* Lila looks down at the bed and at this unrecognizable, almost lifeless person of herself, lying motionless on that bed with the sterilized white, white sheets. She stares at her in disbelief because she can actually see a single tear fall from her eye, and she screams out as loudly as she possibly can, *I want to die, too! I want to die, too! I want to be with my mother,* but her mouth has an endotracheal tube resting inside of her throat. Her harrowing cries remain silent to everyone else but Lila. Her heart aches for the life she had with her mother, as the very special moments of her life flash vividly in front of her. The cardiac monitor above her bed begins to flash colorful warning lights and emitting loud continuous siren-like noises. Lila panics with all of the commotion taking place, ***What is going on? What is happening?*** She sees another nurse wheel in a big red tool box into her room as everyone seems to know just what to do, as hands are moving quickly all over her body from what looks like a dozen or so people wearing these ugly yellow paper gowns. Dr. Hodges suddenly appears. He seems to be a little out of breath, and he yells out very loud to her, *LILA, LILA, don't you dare leave us now. Don't you dare. Come back, Lila. Come back to us, Lila.* Lila's body jolts suddenly and then again. After a few moments of total blackness, she can hear Dr. Hodges say with such an obvious excitement detected in his voice, *She's back! She's back! OK, everyone, Lila is back with us.* Lila then scans the entire room and thinks, ***Are they all crying for me? I see tears coming down from everyone's eyes. How is that possible? I don't even know any of you.*** The room is quiet from almost all noise as Dr. Hodges says in a calm, controlled, but fatherly tone,

> "Welcome back, Lila.
> Welcome back."

Lila feels an indescribable heaviness deep within the walls of her heart. It's a feeling that she is utterly unfamiliar with, but it is almost as comforting as the feeling she experiences when she is at her happiest, but yet sad and loved all at once. Although she is unable to speak with actual words, she conjures up the strength to respond by moving two of her fingers in her right hand as another tear escapes from her eye.

*****

Working in a very busy hospital is full of fast-paced stress, unique challenges and struggles. One can say that it is overwhelming and quite exhausting most days. For the most part, yesterday will be nothing like today. No two days, patients or circumstances, are identical and not quite like your most favorite medical television shows.

***

Samantha Stevens has been a dedicated nurse for over two years now and is very well liked by all of her colleagues, patients, and by everyone who knows her. She is a young ambitious nurse who strives to get through her workday and make a difference in each of her patient's lives. As a floor nurse, mornings are no joke. This all comes at a time when nurses are encouraged to start out their careers on a medical surgical floor to gain the needed experience first before spreading your wings out onto a specialty. As always, Samantha begins her shift before her official start, in hopes of launching a jumpstart on her often-challenging assignment. Being extremely organized is an important quality and attribute for a nurse. It can actually make or break your day. Samantha is very organized. Once her day has been set in motion, she plans out the rest of her shift and hopes that she is not met with any unexpected surprises, *OK, now. Report is finally done. My vital signs, morning rounds, blood sugars and early morning insulins are all done, administered and charted. Now I think after I take my fifteen-minute coffee break, I can begin dispensing my morning medications. But first coffee...*
While standing in front of her medication cart, Samantha reviews her medication administration record for each of her patients. She begins pouring her medication and notices a call bell is ringing from one of her rooms down the end of the hallway, *Oh, I hate for my patients to wait. I hope one of the girls answers it for me,* she thinks as she looks at the light above the door of one of her patient's rooms. She continues to pour her medica-

tion for her patient in her first room and is relieved to see that her nursing assistant has already answered the light and tended to her patient's needs. She goes into her first room, hangs an IV antibiotic, and waits for her patient to swallow the full cup of pills, one at a time, after checking her pulse and blood pressure. Then she pushes her cart toward her next room. A nursing assistant slowly approaches and informs her,

> "Sorry, sweetie, but both of your patients in Room 5 and both in Room 6 are asking for their morning medication now and their pain meds, too.
>
> I told them that you will be in a few minutes because you are in the process of distributing your meds now."

The nursing assistant looks up to see the same call bell on again and says to Samantha,

> "They are ringing again.
>
> I'll go back in and let them know that you are coming."

Samantha sighs and decides to administer the pain meds and morning medications to Room 5 first. She peeks her head into Room 5 and makes the two patients aware that she is on her way to the narcotic cabinet for them, and then does the same for Room 6. While removing pain medication for her patients, the unit secretary notifies Samantha,

> "Sam, I'm sorry,
> but the docs just wrote an order for Room 7 to receive two units of blood today.
>
> The lab is in her room now as we speak, drawing her type and screen.
>
> I'll let you know when her blood is ready.
>
> And oh… sorry, sweetie, but you are up for the next admission, just a heads up."

Samantha smiles and nods at Joanie, the unit secretary, as she thinks, *She is so good. Joanie always keeps me aware of all the new orders that are being written. OK, let me get my meds done in the meantime before the blood is ready and my new admit comes.* She stands in front of her cart pouring the meds before she administers them for both Rooms 5 and then 6 next. She waits as she watches each patient swallow their medication, and then charts that they did. Finally, she moves onto her next room and begins pouring her medication for that room. A visitor from Room 5 walks over to Samantha and begins scolding her for making her mother wait a half an hour for her pain medication. Samantha attempts to explain to the visitor to no avail,

"I am so sorry, but --"

The woman interrupts Samantha abruptly,

"Ah, I am the one talking right now.
It is your job to give my mother her meds on time.
You know, the time it is ordered for.
And I don't care about any of your other patients.
My mother is all I care about.
So unless you want me to make trouble for you,
my mother better be your priority.
In fact, that is what you get paid for."

Samantha realizes, her own mouth is open, *Oops, I could have probably caught a fly just now. Good thing one wasn't in the vicinity.* She closes her mouth and calmly apologizes to the woman. She makes a mental note to herself, *I guess I need to start my med pass with her mother from now on. I can't believe how rude she was with me. I like her mom, too, but I guess she's stressed out about her mom and is taking it all out on me right now. It's not OK, but that excuse will get me through today.* She checks her watch and quickly returns to pouring her meds but is disturbed again by yet another visitor but from Room 7 this time. The woman in her late thirties or early forties stands directly in front of Samantha, bearing a look of complete frustration, and states in a stern voice, trying to get the attention of Samantha,

"Nurse, nurse, nurse."

She clears her throat loudly and repeats herself again and again until Samantha finally diverts her attention from her medication pouring to her. Samantha is trying really hard not be rude, but she is in the middle of pouring liquid medication. She wants to get the correct dose into the cup, which is at her eye level as she pours. The woman becomes quite angry as she huffs, showing her dismay, and says,

"Don't you ignore me, nurse.
I know you can see me."

Samantha puts the medication down on top of the cart and apologizes first before she asks,

"I'm sorry.
I really wasn't ignoring you.
I don't want to make a medication error.
What can I help you with?"

The woman peers straight into Samantha's eyes and explains,

"My father told me that his doctor ordered blood for him.
Why hasn't he received it yet?"

Samantha senses the woman's hostility, but she smiles nervously and calmly replies,

"Oh, yes, the blood is ordered, but it's not ready yet.
The lab will notify us when it's ready for administration."

"But, nurse, what does that mean, "it's not ready"?
This is an emergency.

> Don't you understand?
> If you went to nursing school, you would know that.
> You need to stop stalling and give my father his blood.
> For God's sake, do your job.
> In fact, I'm going straight to administration to report you."

Samantha tries to remain calm and makes a desperate attempt to explain the necessary procedure of blood administration,

> "The lab drew a type and cross screen on your father in order to find a compatible --

The woman quickly turns herself around and deliberately walks away from the nurse, *I am not waiting for this young lazy nurse to give me a bullshit answer. How dare she? Does she think we are all stupid? Hmm, I'll show her,* thinks the woman, as she heads towards administration to report her father's nurse. Samantha is startled at the woman's reaction but again returns to pouring her medication, *OK, now. Where was I? Oh, yeah, that's right.* She rechecks her pouring and is just about ready to walk inside of her patient's room. She begins to step inside of the room, and Joanie calls out to her,

> "Samantha, Samantha, the nursing office is on the phone for you.
> They want to speak with you."

Joanie covers the speaker part of the phone with her hand and adds,

> "Room 7, Mr. Jorgensen's daughter is in the administration office now as we speak making a formal complaint about you.
> And I think she's making a scene down there, too."

Samantha looks toward Joanie, feeling a bit overwhelmed now with her hands full of medication cups. She thinks to herself, *I am never going to finish passing out these meds at this rate. It's almost time to pass noon meds out now.* She then puts down the cup of liquid medication and says,

"Joanie, please tell them I am in the middle of med pass.
I will call them right back after I dispense these meds to this last room."

Now feeling quite frustrated, Samantha walks past Mrs. Stone and hands Mrs. Bedford the small cup of pills. Mrs. Bedford smiles as she admires the colorful array of pills inside of the cup and says,

"Oh…
Did my doctor order something different for me?,"

Hmm, he must have, then she gulps down all the pills from inside of the little cup and chases it with a long sip of water. Samantha then walks back out to her medication cart, and Joanie says as she puts the phone on hold,

"Samantha, they want to speak with you right now."

She instinctively locks her cart and walks over to the phone in front of Joanie. She takes a semi-long deep breath before she explains to administration,

"Hello, this is Samantha."

She listens to the person on the other side of the phone first before she continues to explain,

"I am so sorry, but the blood is not ready yet.
The lab said that they will notify us when the blood is ready for administration.

They are still in the process of cross matching his blood.
My hands are tied for the moment.
I honestly tried to explain this to her,
but she wouldn't listen to me."

Then at that very moment, Samantha feels her heart sink heavily and a wave of nausea suddenly creeps up on her. She can actually feel her blood make the shift as her face turns completely white. She quickly hangs up the phone and pages Mrs. Bedford's intern. Dr. Bae turns off his beeper, as he nonchalantly walks toward the nurses' station from an adjacent patient room asking,

"Who paged me?"

Now completely distraught with fear, Samantha explains to him her dreaded discovery as she cries,

"I accidentally gave Mrs. Bedford her roommate's medication.
It was an accident.
I was distracted and made a med error.
I gave her Mrs. Stone's cardiac and hypertension medications.
I am so, so very sorry.
I shouldn't have allowed myself to become distracted.
Oh my God, I don't want anything to happen to Mrs. Bedford.
Please, help me."

Dr. Bae looks at Samantha. He can see how distressed she is. *She is really upset over this. I've never seen her like this before. She doesn't need a lecture coming from me about this right now*, and replies to her cries as compassionately as he possibly can,

"Samantha, calm down.

It's OK. It's OK.

Let's go and check her vital signs together before I call her attending.

Let me have Mrs. Stone's medication record so that I can see exactly what she was given.

Oh, and Mrs. Bedford's as well, to see if there is a possibility of incompatibility of the medication given with hers.

You reported it right away, and that is extremely important.

We all make mistakes, Samantha.

It's part of being human.

None of us are perfect.

It's just a good thing that you caught it right away."

Dr. Bae and Samantha explain to Mrs. Bedford about the medication error as they check her vital signs. The physician then compares her vital signs with her baseline and thinks, *Good. There is not much of a drop so far in her blood pressure and heart rate from her baseline readings. I think we will have to monitor her more frequently for at least twenty-four hours, but let me run this by her attending first.* Mrs. Bedford smiles and replies kindly to Samantha as she thinks, *Poor child. I think that she is more upset than I am about this whole medication error thing. She hasn't stopped crying and apologizing to me the whole entire time she's been in my room. It was an honest mistake, dear.*

"Oh, dear.

I didn't recognize those pills in the cup, but I took them anyway.

I should have asked you to recheck my meds.

It was clearly an accident, my dear.

Technically, I am just as at fault as you, sweetheart.

Actually, I blame me, not you.

Don't worry yourself so much.

I am quite sure everything will be just fine."

Mrs. Bedford was immediately transferred to the coronary care unit for observation and monitoring as a precaution per her attending orders. Although Samantha had agreed earlier to work a double shift that day as a favor to her manager, but in between her anguish and sobs, she requested to leave work as soon as they could find a replacement for her.

Mrs. Bedford never did suffer from the effects of the medication error other than the inconvenience of being transferred from her room to a cardiac unit for twenty-four hours for observation purposes. Sadly, Samantha never returned to work after that day. No one realized just how distraught and anguished Samantha really was over this error, until the next day when it was too late. To this day, those of us that knew and worked with her, still miss her. Nursing students are taught that nurses should never be disturbed or distracted during med pass because the margin of error is increased substantially, and medication errors are sure to be made. Thirty years later, medication errors and distractions during med pass are still relevant. RIP Samantha.

***

At the end of her long, busy shift, Nurse Mirna exits the elevator and heads toward the employees' entrance. *Oh boy, it looks really cold out there. I should grab a hold of my car keys before I make the trek to my car.* She opens up her handbag and sees the glare of her keys before she reaches inside of her bag. Mirna approaches the doorway and thinks, *It must have snowed during the night. There's a fresh blanket of snow out there. I better get going if I want to make early mass this morning.* She steps outside of the building, making sure to watch her footing. *I don't want to slip and fall. At least the roads are not crowded this early on Sunday mornings.* She steps off of the sidewalk and out onto the street. She is suddenly frightened and lets out a horrific scream, as she is being pulled into a van by a man. *What the hell is going on here?* The man is hanging halfway out of the van, while trying to pull Mirna inside as the driver continues to drive. The man has a firm grasp onto her coat as she kicks, screams and is swinging her arms, wildly attempting to free herself from this stranger.

Adam exits the building. He cannot believe what he is witnessing. His coworker is in obvious trouble, so he runs after the van. He jumps up onto the open side door of the vehicle where Mirna is being dragged from and swings hard at the person holding on to her coat. Mirna is finally freed, as she falls onto the ground, landing on her buttocks. She instinctively puts her hands down to her sides as they become scraped along the street. Adam is relieved that Mirna is free and instinctively jumps off of the van step. His coat gets caught in the door as the driver speeds away, dragging Adam along the way for several blocks before he eventually breaks away.

Hospital security are horrified. They dash out of the building in an attempt to assist their employees as the van reaches the wide open main road and off from hospital property. There is very little traffic on the road this early Sunday morning, but by the time EMS and security reach Adam, the van has already vanished from their sight. In his heroic, selfless act of saving a coworker from harm, Adam sustains numerous internal and external injuries. An hour later, he tragically succumbs to those very same injuries.

Chapter Nine

Infectious Infections and Such

Many doors, specialty areas and avenues, have opened up and expanded in the field of medicine during the past four decades. These doors include nurses. It does makes us all better at what we do in general, but it does increase tunnel vision for those who have bypassed basic Med/Surgical first. Unfortunately, the very distinct door of infection control is wide open. Everyone is exposed to various infectious diseases on a daily basis without ever realizing it. Bacteria, viruses and the world of infection is just everywhere. If you see it, you can wash it off, but if you don't see it, that doesn't mean it isn't there. Scary, isn't it? For those working in a hospital setting, we are all exposed and susceptible to every possible source of disease, viruses, parasites and bacteria, all nicely contained inside one very big building, the hospital.

***

Joey Simonelli lazily rolls out of his bed and slowly shuffles his way into his bathroom. He touches his face and thinks, *What is this? Am I breaking out with pimples or something? It can't be pimples at thirty. I'm too damn old for acne.* He squints his eyes and refocuses his attention by looking up into the mirror and lets out a very loud, *What the hell?* He stares not too long but very hard at his face in complete horror. The recent tingling sensation he felt all around his mouth and cheeks are now bright red and itchy with a few blisters already beginning to form. Total panic, then complete fear, immediately invades Joe's entire body, *This shit is definitely not from shaving,* he thinks as he lightly touches his face. He is not quite sure as to what he should do right now about this rash and decides, *The only thing I can do right now is call our family physician, Dr. Halpern. How embarrassing. He has known me since I was a little boy. He'll know what to do. I think there is something in the doctor laws that says he can't share this delicate, yet personal information with the rest of my family. If this is what I think it is, then I'm completely screwed, big time.*

The receptionist looks up when she hears the door open and waves at Joe, motioning for him to come inside. She immediately opens the door leading inside towards the examination rooms and points toward Exam Room 2 without saying a word. Joe complies, without hesitation, and takes a seat on top of the examination table. He removes his navy blue baseball cap in his futile attempt to hide his facial ugliness from any potential onlookers. He nervously taps his feet while awaiting for someone to enter the room. To Joe, it seemed as though an hour had passed when the door finally opens. Dr. Halpern, a tall, slender gray-haired gentleman wearing a full-length lab coat, slowly enters the room. His easygoing, calm nature, and gentle caring smile hides his initial thoughts as he squints his eyes peering straight ahead in Joey's direction, and specifically at his face. After washing his hands he dons a pair of purple latex-free examination gloves, all while looking at Joey's face. He physically looks over Joey's face before he questions his patient,

"Hmm… OK, Joey.
When did this blistery rash first make its appearance?"

"Well Doc, I woke up with it this morning.
I think I did notice something starting to brew yesterday, but it is horribly worse today.
What the hell is this?"

Dr. Halpern crinkles his forehead and continues to question Joey.

"Joey, do you have this rash anywhere else on your body?"

"No, Doc.
I didn't notice it anywhere else.
So far just on my face, neck and in my mouth, too."

"OK, Joey.
Was there any itching, pain or tingling involved to or around your face before this rash erupted?"

Joey thinks first before he replies,

"As a matter of fact, yes, I did.
Actually, I felt some tingling and itching for a few days before all of this happened.
Does that mean something, doc?
What does this all mean?"

Dr. Halpern sighs fairly long and hard as he removes his gloves and walks toward the sink to thoroughly wash his hands. He jots down a few notes inside of Joey's chart first. He clears his throat and says,

"Joey, this looks like herpes.

Have you recently had questionable or unprotected sex, maybe a week or two ago?"

Now feeling completely embarrassed and fearful all at once, Joey hesitantly but truthfully answers,

"I…, I… I was with a hooker maybe a week or so ago.
We hooked up after my cousin's bachelor party,
but I always wear a condom.
I was drunk out of my mind that night.
Wait… I kind of went down on her.
If you know what I mean?
Shit, I did something real stupid, didn't I?"

"OK, OK, Joey.
This is what we are going to do.
I am going to arrange for you to be admitted into the hospital because of the severity of your symptoms.
We need to treat you aggressively with IV and topical antivirals, pain medication and possibly IV antibiotics.
I am really sorry to tell you this,
but this is a long-term condition, meaning that you may have reoccurring outbreaks now and then.
Let me confer with the head of Infection Control from the hospital first.
This is his specialty, and he will know the best way to treat this.
Wait here a moment.
I'll be right back."

***

Within two hours, Joey solemnly lies on top of his hospital bed, looking up at the ceiling while hooked up to an intravenous bag containing Acyclovir, an antiviral medication. He had noticed two colorful signs taped to the door of his private room when he first entered, *Contact Isolation and Respiratory Isolation.* Joey can't help but to feel slightly ashamed of his dilemma and highly contagious as each hospital staff member who enters his room wears a yellow paper gown, surgical mask, and a pair of gloves before rendering any type of care to him.

Nurse Becky flushes and disconnects the completed intravenous medication from Joey's intravenous lock (intravenous catheter capped off without intravenous fluid), at the end of her shift,

"Joey, I am going off my work shift and into report within a few minutes.

Is there anything you need from me before I go?'

"No, Becky.

Thank you for everything.

Will you be in tomorrow morning?"

Joey replies as he changes the channel on his television.

"Yes, I'll see you tomorrow morning.

Have a good night,"

Becky says. She then removes her PPE equipment, (Personal Protective Equipment) before she washes her hands and heads back to the nurses' station to report off to the oncoming nurse.

***

Carrie Saunders sits in her car waiting and hoping that her daughter Cece and her friends will be walking out of those double doors soon before she is asked to move. *I hope I won't have to drive around the airport again. it's so annoying. Oh good, there they are*, Carrie thinks as she pops open the trunk of her midsize car. Cece walks up to the rear of her mother's car, kisses her mom on the cheek, and swiftly lifts her bag up and into the trunk. Her friends follow suit and hop into the backseat of Carrie's car. Carrie pulls her seatbelt over and successfully clicks the buckle into place and asks, as she carefully maneuvers her way out of her parking spot,

> "How was your trip girls?
> Did you have a good time?
> I must say times have changed.
> For my high school senior trip we went to an amusement park, and we thought that was a big deal.
> You guys went to Mexico.
> Lucky for you, Cece, your mother is super cool, and she let you go,"

Carrie smiles before she giggles at her own joke. Cece looks over towards her mother, then shifts her bottom in her seat again. A single tear escapes from Cece's eye as she shifts herself again and again, feeling terribly uncomfortable, *Shit, it is getting much, much worse. I felt really funny last night. This morning it turned from weird to burning, and now I am in horrific pain. Maybe I have an infection brewing down there, but it is obviously bad `cause I can't take this anymore. I just want this to stop.* She begins to cry, then shouts out loud,

> "Mom, something is terribly wrong with me.
> Take them home, then you have to take me to the doctor right away, please."

Carrie instinctively looks up into her rearview mirror, then quickly at her daughter sitting in the passenger seat,

> "Cece, what is going on?
> What is wrong with you?"

Now with tears streaming down her face, Cece answers,

> "Mom, please don't lecture me.
> I am in excruciating pain… down there."

> "Oh, my God, Cece.
> Did something happen to you in Mexico?

> What happened?
> Tell me now, young lady."

Carrie looks up again into her rearview mirror, but focuses her attention onto the two girls sitting in the back seat of her car,

> "What happened, Gloria?
> Dahlia?
> Somebody better tell me something, and I mean right now."

Feeling slightly nervous and intimidated, Gloria starts out stuttering before she begins crying,

> "W-w-w-well...
> It's kind of my fault because...
> It was my idea to g-g-get a p-p-p-piercing."

That is all Gloria was able to divulge before she starts to cry hysterically. At that point, Carrie can feel her heart pounce outside of her chest as her blood boils over, combining her anger with fear. Her face is now beet red before she screams out,

> "You did what?
> You did what in Mexico?
> In Mexico?"

Cece is in obvious pain with each moan exiting from her mouth. Carrie touches her arm and forehead realizing, *Oh, my God. She is burning up.*

> "Girls, we are all going to the emergency room right now.
> She is burning up.
> You better start telling me everything,
> and I mean everything.
> So what did you guys pierce?
> Just tell me everything, and spare me the crying!"

Cece continues to moan as Gloria weeps, so Dalia sighs, *Shit. I guess I have to tell it all now.*

> "Well, Mrs. Saunders, it's like Gloria said.
> We all went to get a piercing.
> You know, down there."

Now feeling completely frustrated, Carrie says with a more controlled tone in her voice, *I better not yell `cause she might just clam up and not tell me everything. Keep cool, Carrie. Keep cool*,

> "Just tell me, Dahlia.
> I'm already mad, so don't worry about me getting mad.
> Besides I have to know everything so I can explain this to the doctors.
> They need to know the whole truth so they can give her the correct treatment.
> Now spill your guts out."

> "OK, Mrs. Saunders.
> We went to get clit piercings.
> I don't know why.
> I guess we thought it would be exciting or something."

Carrie bites her tongue as she listens to Dahlia explain.

> "Well, Cece kinda went first.
> Then me and Gloria kinda chickened out.
> We couldn't go through with it.
> I'm so sorry.
> We didn't think anything bad would happen.
> It was just a piercing, we thought."

Carrie feels her anger come to a head but takes a very deep breath instead of lashing out like she really wants to. She begins to bargain instead, saying over and over in her mind, *I hope Cece is OK. Please, dear God, let Cece be OK. Please let Cece be OK.*

"Girls, no, I am not mad that you had this ridiculous idea to get a piercing in a third world country.

I cannot find the words to describe how disappointed I am that you went through with this cockamamie (meaning foolish or ridiculous) idea before thinking of what the potential consequences of this action may bring to you.

Mexico is a third world country.

Do you understand what that means?

Then you and Gloria, her good friends, let her go through with this.

I am grateful that you both chickened out as you say, but you should have been better friends to Cece.

You are supposed to look out for each other.

Besides, what do you need with this type of piercing anyway?

Well, that is definitely a conversation for me and Cece to have when she is all better."

Once inside of the emergency room triage area, Cece is quite lethargic, but she continues to moan at a lower volume and in obvious pain. The triage nurse takes one look at her and decides to wheel Cece inside and directly into an exam room. More concerned than embarrassed, Carrie explains to the physician the details told to her from Gloria and Dahlia. The emergency room attending, Dr. Herman, listens intently while the nurse prepares Cece for an examination of her pelvic area, obtains and records her vital signs, draws labs and starts an intravenous line before Carrie even completes her version of the second-hand story. The experienced nurse works quickly and efficiently as she listens to Carrie and thinks, *OK, I drew a CBC (complete blood count), and a CMP (complete metabolic panel). She is febrile, and while listening to her mother's story, I think I better get blood cultures, too.* Dr. Herman notices the nurse is ready for him, and he immediately washes his hands at the sink in the corner of the room. He looks compassionately towards Carrie and states,

> "I think that it would be best if you wait outside during the examination.
> We will call you right back in as soon as we are done, if you like?"

Carrie nods, unable to smile, and she hesitantly makes her way back to Gloria and Dahlia who are both sitting in the waiting room area.

Dr. Herman dons a pair of examination gloves as the nurse assists him with the pelvic exam. Cece continues to moan in pain in between sobs, but is still able to answer questions coherently despite her increasing lethargy. The nurse gently pulls back Cece's patient gown, along with the cover drape across her legs, exposing the affected area. Dr. Herman's dark brown eyes widen at the site before him as he thinks to himself in a visually discreet horror, ***WOW... I can see why she is febrile (Having a fever) and in dire pain. Ouch...*** The nurse looks down at Cece's pubic area first, and then she quickly, but briefly, focuses her attention towards the attending physician and thinks, ***Ah, he has the same thoughts as I do; that looks really painful***. She quietly watches as she observes the emergency room attending gently remove the piercing from the normally sensitive area that is now the size of a baseball, as red as a tomato, and obviously completely infected. She holds an open sterile container in front of Dr. Herman, he nods as he drops the small hoop inside of it. He then irrigates the area with a warm sterile, normal saline solution, before applying a warm compress to help promote drainage of the purulent discharge oozing out. Not a word is spoken between the two professionals, but they nod in agreement as if they already knew what the other is thinking. He looks at the nurse and thinks to himself, ***I can see we are on the same page here. We need to focus on getting her stable right now before she becomes septic,*** then he refocuses his thoughts and says,

"I'll put the orders in now for her, but let's get her something for pain; Morphine 2mg IVP, (intravenous push) and a Tylenol suppository 650mg for her fever STAT and Q6 hours PRN (every 6 hours, when necessary).

Draw a CBC, CMP and blood cultures X2.

Let's send a urinalysis and a urine pregnancy test to the lab STAT.

You can place a foley catheter, if you think you need to.

Oh, and let's give her some fluids IV, too.

Her mother says Cece has no known allergies that they know of.

After all the labs are drawn, we'll start her on IVAB, (intravenous antibiotics) most likely an antibacterial agent.

I'll call ID (Infectious Disease) now and see what his recommendations are for her.

I'd better call her gynecologist too for that matter, as he thinks to himself, *They may want to do an I&D and drain the area*.

I'm sure we'll be able to get a bed for her up in pediatrics. She's just eighteen.

Then I'll go and talk to her mother and update her on everything so far.

I'll be at the desk putting in her orders, if you need me."

The nurse looks at Cece with a compassion, she has done so many times with her own teenage daughter, as she calmly explains the physician orders to her, while trying to make her a little more comfortable. The compassion in her heart is extended not only to Cece but to her mother as well. The old school nursing professional almost literally takes a bite into her own tongue thinking, *Girl, now what were you thinking? Oh, that's right. It's sort of a passage right for young teenage girls to do something exciting and daring and something our parents would absolutely hate. Not all kids act on this urge, but the ones who do seem to get more and more creative at this rebellion thing. Well, I'm sure you have just learned a very valuable lesson today. But ouch, girl! You picked the most sensitive area in your body to experiment and explore with. Ohhh, the pain! Maybe an umbilical piercing would have been a little less painful and possibly a little less embarrassing as well. But I give your mom loads of cudos. She handled herself well and brought you straight in. Better than most parents I have had the pleasure of coming in contact with over the years. And I most certainly have witnessed different reactions from many parents that have ended up getting themselves kicked out of the emergency department and even worse. OK, young lady, let's draw that second set of blood cultures on you. Oh, good, it looks like the Morphine is finally kicking in now.*

***

Danny Jones drove himself to the emergency room, holding his left hand up high above his heart, and thinks to himself, *I read somewhere that the wound needs to be above your heart. It needs to be held above your heart, above the heart,* he kept telling himself out loud the whole way there. He actually felt some sort of comfort hearing his own voice out loud over and over again. The emergency department security guard notices Danny's hand is meticulously padded and heavily wrapped in a plain white hand towel and taped with surgical gauze, probably from a first aid kit. He first sees Danny stroll through the automatic doors with his left hand held up in the air. His attention is then immediately diverted to his non-affected hand holding a clear plastic baggie filled with ice and something else wrapped inside, what he surmises to be a washcloth. Chris Apostle has been working security for the past ten years with the same hospital after completing two tours of duty in the military. Chris curiously walks up to Danny to question him while thinking, *I've seen a lot of crazy and wild things pass through these doors over the years, but I'd bet everything I own, he has a finger inside of there,*

"Sir, what do you have inside of the bag?"

Danny answers gratefully as he thinks, ***Oh, good. I didn't know what to do next after entering those doors. At least he knows if they will take me inside right away or not,***

"I accidentally cut my finger off.
I'm a butcher.
My finger is actually inside of this bag of ice."

Without hesitation or a change in his normal cheery demeanor, Chris quickly grabs a wheelchair for Danny. He then pokes his head into the triage room and notifies the nurse regarding Danny's situation. The triage nurse looks directly into Chris' eyes and quickly concludes to herself, ***Oh... He's not joking***, then immediately wheels Danny inside beyond the doors of waiting to be seen STAT (immediately) by the surgical team.

Once inside the inner sanctity of the emergency department, the surgical team consisting of residents, interns, PAs, and nurses, methodically prepares Danny for microsurgery and reattachment of a severed digit. The emergency surgical attending, Dr. D... calls in a plastic surgeon while his team works together drawing labs, recording Danny's surgical and medical history, obtaining a complete physical assessment, and administer tetanus before sending Danny to the pre-op holding area on a gurney. Dr. Victor, the plastic surgeon, is already awaiting for the arrival of Danny into pre-op holding. An IV is immediately inserted by anesthesia and IV antibiotics administered, all while Dr. Victor explains the entire procedure to Danny. Consent is then obtained and signed before Danny is wheeled into the operating room and Dr. Victor scrubs in for the surgery.

Danny is feeling completely exhausted and lucky. *It certainly has been a very long traumatizing day for me. All in the life of a butcher, I suppose. Shit, I have to stop daydreaming while I work. I really hope this surgery worked,* thinks Danny as his gurney stops in front of a bed on a post-surgical unit. The nursing staff readily assists Danny onto his bed as he thinks, while quickly scanning the room, *Nice private room. I need to get some sleep, but I guess I have to answer questions first from the nurses here. They are calling me a, "New Admission."* Stephanie, Danny's night nurse, props his arm up on top of several pillows above his heart, as she looks over his surgical dressing and checks his radial pulse. *Hmm, good. Strong, bounding pulses. Vitals are within normal limits, low dose IV Heparin patent with correct dose infusing well. IV sites are healthy. OK then. I think we are done for now,* she mentally sums everything up as she finishes up her physical assessment of Danny.

> "Mr. Jones, I am done with my assessment.
> You had your pain medication already.
> It looks like you can reach everything you may need, unless you would like me to move your table a little more closer to you?"

Danny smiles and shakes his head no before he answers,

> "Thank you, Stephanie.
> I'm fine for now.
> Please call me Danny.
> My father is Mr. Jones."

Stephanie chuckles before she responds,

> "OK then, Danny.
> I'll be in several times during the night to check in
on you.
> I promise not to wake you.
> Call us if you need anything at all, OK?"

Danny returns the smile and lets the heaviness of his eyelids completely take over his entire body while Stephanie quietly closes the door behind her. His breathing is light and easy, even though they encouraged him to keep the nasal cannula on for the night. *To keep me well oxygenated is what I think they told me,* his mind wanders back to the surgery, just hours ago. *Wow, that reattachment of my finger was actually quite amazing. After they stuck that needle into my back, I didn't feel a thing. I was awake for the whole entire time just watching through those cameras and hearing everything that was going on. The anesthesiologist had a drape in front of everything, but I had front row seats to it all. I can't get over the notion that I didn't even feel anything at all. It was really, really great. But thinking back to what brought me here in the first place, what a dummy I am. Now I can only hope it all works,* is the very last thing Danny remembers thinking before he finally drifts off into a deep slumber.

Allison Henson takes notes and listens quietly as the night nurse Stephanie reports off to her,

> "In 403 is Danny Jones.
> He's a 43-year-old, white male.
>
> No known allergies, with no past medical or surgical history to talk about, except for an appendectomy (surgical removal of appendix), as a child.
>
> He is now post op Day 1 for reattachment of a severed digit.
>
> It was his left index finger.
>
> He has the original surgical dressing to his left hand in place. It is dry and intact with no visible signs of drainage noted.
>
> From the pictures in his chart, you can see that it was a very nice, clean cut.
>
> He's a butcher by trade who accidently severed his own finger.
>
> He then immediately drove himself to the emer-

gency room.

Low dose heparin is infusing well at 10ml per hour via an 18-gauge angiocath in his right forearm from the O.R., labeled and dated.

He also has an 18-gauge saline lock in his right AC for his IVABs (intravenous antibiotics), also from the O.R.

His surgeon is Dr. Victor, so he is followed by plastics.

Dr. V's orders for today include… ah… leech therapy.

He'll be in for the first dressing change probably after his early morning scheduled surgery.

I asked around because I wasn't sure where you can get leeches from for today's treatment.

Pharmacy will have them for you.

I believe that Dr. V's team alerted pharmacy to order them for Mr. Jones' treatment.

You know that Plastics likes to do the first surgical dressing change, but you should have everything ready for them."

Stephanie hands over a medium-size brown cardboard box neatly filled with various items to Allison and adds,

"I think I have everything here in this box you will need for the dressing change except for the leeches and pain medication, of course.

But check the box and add anything you think they may want or need.

You know he is very picky, so I did include several extra sterile gowns, sterile gloves, and his special surgical kit is in the box, too."

Allison looks at Stephanie with a bewildered look on her face and asks curiously,

"Ah, what exactly is leech therapy?
I don't have to touch them, do I?"

"Well, Allison, I never actually did it myself, but I did a little bit of research for you.

They are blood suckers that also secrete peptides and proteins used to prevent blood clotting and promote circulation.

It seems that it is a method widely used by plastic surgery and microsurgery for specific vascular needs.

Pharmacy says that you place them on the affected area, allowing them to latch on and let them do their job.

When they are full and fat, they will actually fall off from the area they were attached to.

Then you place the full ones into a sterile container and return them back to pharmacy.

I would definitely wear gloves during that treatment.

I don't envy you, sweetie.

I hope you have a great day.

I'm back tonight.

See you tonight.

Then you can tell me all about it."

Allison sighs as she thinks to herself, *Sounds pretty gross, but I am kind of curious to see how this all works. Little bloodsuckers.*

"Thank you so much, Stephanie for getting everything ready for me.

But honestly I am not looking forward to touching and handling those leeches.

The word leeches is gross enough all by itself.

But I guess it will be a new experience for me.

I never imagined that being a nurse I would be required to touch leeches.

Blood, guts and poop, yes, but never leeches.

Thanks again, honey.

See you tonight.

Get home safe, Stephanie."

Dr. Victor makes his way to the nurses station and asks,

"Good morning, ladies.
Which nurse has my patient Danny Jones today?"

"I do, Doctor.
There is actually a box of supplies inside of his room for you.
I think that it has everything you may need for his dressing change except for the leeches, of course.
Is there anything specific you need?"

Allison replies as she hands him Danny's medical chart. He quickly looks over the orders written by the chief surgical resident and states,

"I'll be in his room.
Can you meet me in his room with the leeches?
Oh, is he due for his pain medication?
If he is, then bring that in with you too, OK?"

"He was medicated last about twenty minutes ago, Doctor.
I just have to run down to pharmacy and pick up the leeches.
I'll meet you in his room with them.
Just give me a few minutes."

She takes a deep breath standing in front of the door before she actually enters Danny's room. **OK, girl. Catch your breath. It wasn't that far a walk to the pharmacy,** she thinks while holding a clear plastic container holding a half dozen leeches. Allison holds the container at eye level first, *Yuk. Ugly parasitic wormlike bloodsuckers.* Dr. V had already undressed Danny's finger and hand dressing. Allison places the container down on the bedside table. She strategically positions herself on the opposite side of Danny, giving herself a clear view of the wound. Dr. Victor carefully lays out and explains his plans and expectations for Danny over the next few days. Her eyes are quickly fixated onto Danny's finger, *Wow. The suturing is so very fine that I can barely see them. His finger is a little bit swollen and maybe a little off color, but attached. It is basically the very top portion of his finger that was amputated. It really looks pretty good.* Dr. V cannot help but to smile as he notices the expression written all over Allison's face, then says,

"It looks pretty good, doesn't it?"

Allison nods in agreement but is afraid to make any comments at this moment, thinking, *Oh, no. He's getting ready to show me how to do the leeches now. Yuk. He's looking at me. That is coming next, I know it. OK, just smile and try not to look creeped out over the bloodsuckers. Breathe Allison. Ahh, it will be fine.*

The surgeon now continues to smile and tries desperately to hold in a chuckle that desperately wants to escape while he peers at Allison from the corner of his eye. He then calmly explains the procedure of leech therapy to his patient and Allison as he slips on a pair of exam gloves,

"Now all you do is pick up one leech at a time and place them over here.
Wait until they latch onto the affected area.
You can put a few on at a time.
Once they are full, they will fall off.
This procedure will aide in promoting circulation to the area, allowing it to heal.
I have ordered this to be done BID, (twice daily)."

Danny quietly watches in amazement as the leeches work diligently attached to his finger, *Look at those little leeches work. It's crazy. I don't even feel a thing right now. I can see them, but I don't feel them on top of my finger. I believe he said that I may, or may not get the feeling back into that finger, but it's too early to tell anything yet. Maybe after the swelling is gone and the sutures are out. Oh, but I think he said something about the nerve endings, too.*

Allison doesn't say or breathe a word immediately after Dr. V leaves the room, *Hmm, I guess he is on his way to the nurses' station to dictate and update his progress notes on his patient. Actually… I don't think I really need to stay here and watch this whole procedure to be completed. I can come back in a few minutes and collect all the little fallen buggers. I just may be able to pass out a few more medications in the meantime.* She notices that Danny is now completely fascinated as he watches his little tribe of leeches fill up their bellies on his finger. A completely satiated leech falls off onto the white towel nicely laid out underneath Danny's arm and completely covering the top of his table. Allison squeamishly picks it up with a gloved hand, then drops it into an empty specimen container next to Danny's arm. Danny gleefully watches Allison's facial expressions, *Yuk. I have a glove on and it still feels slimy. Oops, I hope that my face doesn't give away what I'm feeling,* and he then offers a suggestion,

> "Nurse, I know you are busy and have other patients to care for besides me.
>
> There is no need for both of us to watch this thing through.
>
> Just help me place a glove onto my free hand and when they fall off, I can easily drop them into the container.
>
> If you like, I can call for you when they are all done."

Now feeling quite relieved, she ponders, *Oh, yessss… I am most certainly happy that he offered to pick up those nasty little parasites. It is definitely a guy thing. They are the ones who like touching bugs and worms and such. I don't mind picking them up and running them back down to the pharmacy after each treatment. Yuk, yuk and gross on touching them, though. But if I have to do it, I will.* Allison smiles and replies as she washes her hands before helping glove Danny's right hand,

"OK, thank you.

I would like to ask Dr. V a question and review his physician orders as well before he physically leaves the unit.

I will be back in fifteen minutes."

***

Mr. Sing sits in the large sleeper chair beside his wife of thirty-five years. His fingers gently touches a small portion of her hand over and over that is unaffected by the purplish eruptions that has mysteriously infiltrated most of her body from head to toe. His eyes are red and swollen from either crying or lack of sleep or possibly both. His heart is broken as he helplessly watches his love and best friend suffer needlessly, *Why, why, must she suffer? Why must she suffer like this? She just had a cold and now this? Why?* Lena, their oldest daughter, takes over her father's diligent stand of, *never leaving his wife's bedside so that her mom will never be left alone.* With much persuasion, Lena has finally convinced her father to go home for a few hours a day,

"Dad, mom would want you to shower.

You know that.

So, please, let Richie take you home so you can shower, eat and take a nap, please.

Mom wouldn't want you to get sick, too."

Reluctantly her father concedes and allows Lena's husband Richie drive him home. Tears well up in Lena's eyes as she looks around her mother's room in the highly sanitized burn unit. She takes over her father's seat and gently slips her hand underneath her mother's hand as she listens to the even, controlled rhythm of the machine responsible for her mother's breathing. Her eyes then glance over to the monitor above the bed with different colors that represent her mother's vital signs; green for her heart rate, red for her blood pressure, blue for her respirations, white for her oxygen saturation, and a few other numbers and colors that she is unsure of their actual meaning. She leans over slightly towards her mother and whispers,

> "Mama, I am here.
> I am here with you.
> Don't worry about pop.
> Richie and I will take care of him.
> He's still as stubborn as ever, but I convinced him to go home for a bit.
> I know that you would want him to take care of himself.
> We are here for you mama.
> We want you to get better and come home.
> We will always be by your side mama.
> We love you."

Lena fights the urge to cry thinking, *I need to be strong. I need to be strong like you are mom, but I need to be strong for you now. Hmm, they really could have picked a prettier color for these ugly yellow paper gowns. Maybe a lavender color to go with the pretty purple gloves they make us wear, too. Look at me trying to color coordinate the PPE equipment for the burn unit.* The sudden collection of various colored scrubs catches her attention from the corner of her eye. Lena looks up to see the burn unit staff standing outside of her mother's room through the plexiglass walls, *Oh, they must be making their morning rounds. The doctor told me yesterday that mom is in for the long haul of a recovery with this Steven Johnson Syndrome. I don't understand how this can happen to someone. He said that mom probably had a reaction to the antibiotics given to her by her physician. She insisted on receiving an antibiotic for her upper respiratory infection, but she neglected to tell him that she had been taking a bunch of healing herbs as well. He said that they suspect she had a drug interaction between her prescribed antibiotic and her herbal medications. I think that she didn't realize herbs are included as medication when they ask you about your medication history.*

The severity of Mrs. Sing's condition is so extreme that began with fever, a skin rash that blistered and peeled over her entire body including her mucous membrane, but she does know that her daughter Lena is here with her, *I can feel your hand, Lena. I may be in a medically induced coma, is what I heard them say, but I hear, smell and feel you beside me my dear child. My poor husband is suffering along with me, too... They said that I became septic as a complication of all of this. I feel as though my whole body is on fire from the inside out, is the only way I can explain this. Why did this happen to me? What have I done that is so terrible to deserve this? I can hear them all talking about me. I am here. I am right here. I am trapped inside of my body that seems to be having a war within my body, and I cannot do anything about it. Will I survive this war?* A few tears escape down the sides of Mrs. Sing's face, landing on her pillow, but no one notices.

Chapter Ten

All Tied Up

Change and progress is inevitable regardless of profession. We learn, we evolve, and we progress to bigger and better changes. The field of medicine and nursing are no different. Finding cures and better ways to deliver safe, effective cares for our patients, community and families are what we work, strive and live for. Working as a nurse in the seventies was a new fun, intriguing experience for a young nurse. The eighties brought excitement to the mix. In the nineties, the young nurse now had twenty years of experience under her belt. Twenty years became thirty and thirty became forty. She looks back at her very long career and she now has become that old nurse she remembers who told her old war stories of how it used to be way back when. She remembers using the Brewer system, that eventually became the Pyxis (automated medication dispensing system). Paper charting became electronic charting, and she embraced it. Scanning medications, unit doses, satellite pharmacy, primary care, teamwork, modules, teams, critical thinking, restraint vests, and etcetera... and etcetera... and etcetera...

***

Old Charley O'Connor is how everyone in the neighborhood described him. Except Old Charley wasn't as old as he looked. He spent most of his thirties in and out of various local hospitals recouping from ailments stemming from his many years of drinking. Eventually Charlie became known as one of many *"Frequent Flyers,"* amongst the emergency department staff because of his numerous hospital admissions with diagnoses of hepatic failure (liver failure) and hepatic encephalopathy (a decline in brain function as a result of liver failure), multiple trauma from falls and so forth. In general, the staff liked Charley. He was pleasant and funny and it was extremely difficult to watch him decline.

His decline eventually left him completely incapable of caring for himself at any level. During the early eighties, nurses were able to physically restrain patients for their own protection with the blessing from a physician. Unfortunately, restraining Charley no longer became an option for the nursing staff. He rolled out of bed onto the floor, fell frequently and was found in other patient rooms repeatedly. He could no longer comprehend or follow simple directions and ultimately became a danger to himself and to others. His focus was always, *Can I have a drink and a cigarette*? Back in the day, nurses would apply a vest restraint around Charley's chest and tie it behind his chair while he sat in the hallway in front of his room. His room was usually in front of the nurses' station so they could watch over him as closely as possible; besides he did enjoy the company of the staff. As the nursing staff run up and down the hallways, in and out of patient's rooms working, the dialogue between Charley's slurred speech and the nursing staff was always,

> "Hey, Charley.
> Are you OK?
> Do you need to go to the bathroom yet, Charley?"

> "Hey, h-h-how are you nursey?
> Do ya have a drink for me h-h-honey?"

> "Sure, Charley, do you want apple juice or water?"

> "Nah, how about a s-s-s-shot of whiskey?
> Do ya have that for me?

I can really use a drink and a cigarette."

Sometimes you can hear Charley muttering to himself, *Damn, what kind of establishment is this? Can't a patron get a lousy drink? This is the last time I'm coming to this bar.*

Social services had a difficult job finding placement in a long-term care facility for Charley, so he became a temporary resident of the hospital until then. Charley sat in his usual spot most days. Visitors became accustomed to his presence, and Charley always said hello to everyone as they passed by him,

> "Hey, there.
> G-g-g-got a drink?
> H-h-h-how about a knife?"

As he shimmied his bottom around in his chair while trying to free himself.

> "Hey, you over there,
> do ya h-h-have a knife or a scissor?
> I'm stuck here in this chair.
> If I had a knife or a scissor, I can get myself unstuck here."

A young couple in their early twenties stop in front of Charley and giggle before they visit a friend down the hallway. Charley says,

> "Hey, do ya have a knife or a scissor on ya?"

They smile and giggle some more as they shake their heads no. Charley then asks,

> "OK, then.
> H-h-how about a cigarette and a light for your old friend?"

Without hesitation, the young man pulls out a single cigarette from a pack he carried inside of his jacket pocket, along with a book of matches. He giggles as he hands them over to

Charley. His girlfriend whispers to him, *I don't think that's a good idea. You shouldn't have given that to him.* He smiles and whispers back to her, *Ah, why not? But let's get out of here before someone sees us talking to him.* The couple hurry down the hallway as Charley yells out to them,

"Hey, thanks buddy!"

Charley smiles, looking at the cigarette, **Hmm, looks like a Marlb -- ciggy. I think I used to smoke them,** and then his attention is refocused from the cigarette to the book of matches, **This should work out just fine.** He places the cigarette down on top of his lap. **OK, now. Let's see. Let's light this bad boy up now,** he thinks as he attempts to light a match. **Nope. Nothing. Let's try another one. Ah, yes, success,** on his third and final attempt. His hand dexterity has been slowly declining over the past few years, so he drops the lit match on top of his chest vest restraint. He looks down at his chest and is immediately frightened by the orange flame dancing freely on top of his chest. He begins to yell out loud as it spreads,

"Fire, Fire, Fire!
Help, help, Help!
Fire, Fire, Fire!"

A nursing assistant hears Charley yelling as she exits from a room only two doors away. She lets out a shriek at an unlikely sight, flames on her patient's chest. Instinctively, she quickly throws the blanket she held in her hands on top of Charley's chest as she continues to scream for help, in her selfless attempt to extinguish the fire. The entire staff immediately responds to her shrieks as nurses, assistants and physicians rush to the scene. Most of the visitors are now gathering in the hallways outside of the patient rooms curiously watching in horror as the fire is completely smothered, and Charley is quickly transferred to the hospital's burn unit with second degree burns to his chest, hands and neck. The physician rummages through the smoke and smells of fresh burning flesh. He notices the cigarette and matches and wonders, *Where did he get these from? Who in their right mind would give him a cigarette and matches to boot?* As Charley is being transferred off of the floor, the physician questions his patient.

> "Charley, where did you get the cigarette and the matches from?
> Did someone give them to you?"

Even in obvious physical pain, Charley smiles and replies,

> "Oh, yeah, my buddy gave them to me.
> Him and his girl.
> I asked him if he had a ciggy and a match.
> He said sure and gave them to me.
> Nice guy, he is.
> Buddy."

The physician looks around and then down the hall toward the various visitors standing around talking amongst each other as they curiously watch Charley and the staff. He notices a young couple standing around and thinks to himself, *I wonder if that's Charley's buddy and his girl over there. Even if it was them, I'm sure they would deny it anyway. They actually look guilty. It's all written in their body language.*

I suppose everyone doesn't wear their heart on the left side of their chest. His attention is then immediately returned to his patient Charley as he moans uncomfortably,

> "It's OK, Charley.
> We're going to take good care of you."

He takes a hold of Charley's hand as the transporter and nurse guides the gurney onto the elevator.

"*Buddy*," quietly watches as Charley is being wheeled down the hall and off of the unit. *Oh shit. The old man really did set himself on fire. Crazy old Charley,* he thinks to himself. His girlfriend looks at him with the dirtiest look she could muster up at that moment and whispers into his ear, *You Jerk off. Maybe you shouldn't have given him the matches. Obviously, he was tied to the chair for a good reason. You never use that brain of yours to think or to listen to me.*

***

Mary Vincente lay tired and motionless in intensive care unit
Bed 2, surrounded by her three daughters and two of her sons. The machine beside her bed continues its rhythmic breathing for her; a long whoosh one, whoosh two, whoosh three, to a total of twelve breaths per minute. Her children sit and observe the readings displayed on the cardiac monitor above her bed. A nurse quietly slips into the dimly lit room to exchange the almost completed intravenous bag for a full one, then according to her routine, checks her patients' vital signs. She tries desperately to work quietly and quickly as to not disturb Mary's children. Francie, the oldest daughter, gently strokes her mother's hair. Her heart aches with mostly concern over her mother's condition, ***Mom you have to get better. We need you.*** She carefully leans over and whispers into her mother's ear, *We are all here for you, mom; me, Judy, Nancy, Carlo, and Tony. We are always here for you and we love you.* Francie then takes her mother's hand and squeezes it as she addresses her siblings once the nurse exits the room,

> "You see,
> mom knows we are here.
> She just squeezed my hand, I'm sure of it."

Everyone smiles as the conversation amongst them continues. Mary feels a sense of relief knowing all of her children are together by her bedside, ***Family. My family. That is the most important thing in the world to me. My children are all here with me.***

But wait a minute, where's Benny? She didn't say Benny was here.
Her heart suddenly races with concern as the cardiac monitor's
warning bell sounds off, indicating her heart rate slightly exceeds the parameters set by the staff.

The warning bells inside of the room averts all eyes to the
monitor above their mother's bed. Francie alerts the nurse by
pressing her mother's call bell. A nurse looks inside of the room
and Francie says excitedly,

> "Didn't you hear the bells going off, nurse?
> Something is wrong with our mother."

Sensing the high anxiety in her patient's room, the nurse answers calmly,

> "We are able to see the monitors out in the nurses'
> station and --

Francie rudely cuts her off,

> "Then why didn't you get your "A" in here?
> My mother could be dying."

Francie continues to ramble on when her brother Carlo interrupts her,

> "Francie, let the nurse finish first.
> Sorry, nurse, my sister can get very excitable."

The nurse smiles and continues,

> "We can hear the bells and warning signs for all of
> the patients in the unit at the nurses' station.
> We set the alarms to go off as an alert for us.
> Your mom's heartrate did slightly exceed the
> parameters we had set it at.
> That is what the warning told us.
> There were not any other changes.
> It did not indicate a reason for immediate attention.
> As you can see, the warning bells has already

stopped.

They will go on and off now and then.

But, again, we are able to see what is going on at the station.

Of course, if you do have any concerns, I am here to answer your questions."

Francie sighs before she apologizes,

"Sorry, nurse.

I'm just worried about my mother.

She is my only concern.

I didn't mean anything by my remarks."

The nurse smiles, nods her head, and before she leaves the room she replies,

"I understand."

The siblings sink all the way back into their seats, realizing the nurse was right. The only sound to be heard now is coming from the respirator. The alarms had stopped. Although their anxiety and concerns over their mother's condition are warranted, but perhaps not to the extent for which they have just displayed, is the main topic being discussed amongst the siblings when the door opens. A tall, looming figure stands at the doorway. The atmosphere in the hospital room immediately changes at the sight of this individual. Francie frees her mother's hand as she jumps to her feet and lets out a cry heard throughout the unit,

"Benny, get the hell out of here!

You are not welcomed here!"

Benny retaliates, as he has done so many times in his life,

"What the hell, Francie!

Why wasn't I told?

Mom is in the hospital and no one tells me?

All of you knew?
She is my mother, too.
I should have been notified of her condition."

The small chatter throughout the intensive care unit comes to a sudden halt. All eyes are now diverted toward Room 2 and the obvious commotion taking place within the room. Dr. Cordova, a third year surgical resident, slowly walks towards Room 2 in an attempt to deescalate the heated family discussion saying,

"Everyone, please calm down.
This is a hospital, and you are disturbing the other patients on the unit."

The six foot two, three hundred-thirty pound Benny angrily whisks his body around and yells out loud,

"You mind your own damn business,"

first before he balls his right hand up into a fist and takes a full swing at Dr. Cordova, hitting him square in his face. Mary's nurse immediately recognized trouble brewing the moment Benny entered the unit through the double doors. Her instinctive fears were now confirmed as she makes a report on the phone to the emergency police hotline. Her colleagues had already notified hospital security and administration while the remainder of the staff ran to Dr. Cordova's side after the force of Benny's fist threw the unsuspecting physician up a few feet into the air and well across the room.

Benny's brothers, Tony and Carlo, jump up out of their seats to constrain their older brother, a familiar task at family gatherings. Francie grabs Benny around his neck as if to place him into a chokehold while sisters, Nancy and Judy, cheerlead in the sidelines. The double doors suddenly open up to the chaos taking place on the other side. Allen, the nursing administrator's initial reaction is, ***What the -- is going on in here!*** He takes a quick moment to analyze the pandemonium going on before his eyes and immediately recognizes the point of inception. His military and nursing background combined, along with four huge security guards, easily helps in the aid of taking control of the entire situation even before law enforcement arrives to the scene.

The Vincente family is quickly disassembled and gathered into a conference room situated at the far end of the unit. Each member does as they are told and takes a seat at the conference table as Allen enters the room. He addresses the family first,

> "Now, we are going to discuss this calmly like adults.
> Only one person at a time will be allowed to speak.
> So, who would like to explain to me the facts only of what just happened here?"

Benny begins speaking first after clearing his throat,

> "Ahem, I just found out that mother has been hospitalized.
> She's been here for a few days already, and no one has informed me of anything."

Francie is about to scream out in retaliation to Benny's comments when Judy grabs ahold of her arm as she watches Allen's demeanor. So she quickly calms herself down before she replies,

> "Well, none of us are speaking to you because you are an "A,"
> but the hospital should have notified you anyway. It's their job to notify the family."

Allen interrupts them both and says,

> "OK, I see what is going on here.
> I have already reviewed your mother's chart, and we have Francie reported as the next of kin and emergency contact for her.

There is also documentation indicating Francie accompanied her into the hospital on the day she was admitted.

Am I right?"

Without saying a word, all family members, except for Benny, nod their heads in agreement. Allen then continues with his explanation,

"We encourage large families, such as yourselves, to appoint one family member to be the spokesperson and the contact person for their loved one.

We are obligated to only notify one member of the family for any changes in the patient's condition.

It is not up to us to call every single member of the family.

It is up to the person known as the emergency contact or spokesperson to notify the rest of the family members themselves.

Whatever your family problems or dynamics are, keep that at home.

Please be forewarned that the outrageous behavior and outburst displayed here today in the Intensive Care Unit will not be tolerated ever again.

So please do not force us to prohibit visitation rights to anyone in your family.

We do not like doing that to anyone, but this behavior of yours put my staff and our patients' safety at risk today.

We cannot have that.

I will personally enforce restrictions and call law enforcement if you entertain even a thought of engaging in this type of behavior again in the future.

I hope that I have made myself very clear on this matter."

The siblings nod their heads yes again in acknowledgement.

Carlo scans the room with his eyes only and thinks to himself, *I have never in my entire life seen my family this quiet, ever.* Two law enforcement officers suddenly appear at the doorway of the conference room and ask,

"We are looking for the nursing administrator. We were told he was in here."

Allen immediately introduces himself to the officers and thanks them for responding,

"Gentleman, thank you for responding to our call."

They continue,

"We understand that there was a disturbance and an assault reported here."

Allen responds to the officers,

"That is correct, sir.
But as you can see, we now have everything under control.
I have spoken to the person who was assaulted, and we have decided not to press charges or file a complaint at this time.
I hope that this will not be a problem."

The two officers smile and say,

"Not at all.
We already spoke with Dr. Cordova, and you just confirmed what he told us.
But we did tell him.
If he ever has a reason to change his mind, we will be more than happy to oblige.
Thank you, folks.
Now I hope you all have a nice quiet rest of your evening."

The two officers smile, while intentionally showing their teeth, before they slowly walk toward the elevators. Then they nod their heads in unison as they tip their caps up to the staff on their way out of the unit and through the double doors.

CHAPTER ELEVEN

The Final Chapter

Screams of *help, help, help, nurse help, help, help,* echo eerily and are unmistakably coming from the very last room on the left side of the long hallway. The screams emerge almost ear piercingly loud from this petite five-foot-tall, middle-aged woman paid by family to watch over Belinda Morgan. The staff arrive to find Belinda unresponsive but completely dressed sitting on top of the lid of the toilet seat. The first nurse, Colleen, enters the room and notices Belinda's arm is extended out on top of the sink's countertop. A tourniquet is tightly wrapped around Belinda's extended upper arm with the needle still halfway inserted into her vein from an empty syringe. The rest of the staff members follow quickly and instinctively grab and push the large red crash cart all the way down the corridor. The code alert is heard throughout the building over the loud speaker as the code team enters the room. The chief medical resident, Jeannie Barnum, is the first physician to enter the room. Her attention is immediately alerted to the two familiar, experienced nurses administering rescue breaths and chest compressions to what appears to be a middle-aged woman sprawled out on her back of the floor outside of the bathroom. Nurses Colleen and Denise carefully, but quickly, pulled Belinda down and off of the toilet seat then onto the floor in order to initiate CPR to their patient. Then they dragged her just outside of the bathroom past the doors before continuing with alternating chest compressions and rescue breaths again. The chief listens while another nurse reports off their findings, as she calls out her orders to the team,

> "Do we have a usable line on her?
> OK, administer Naloxone 2mg."

The nurse at the crash cart had anticipated this order and readily hands it off to a nurse closest to the patient. Then on the count of three, five staff members simultaneously lift Belinda up off of the floor and onto her bed. They quickly roll her onto her side and place the removable headboard underneath the upper portion of her torso. Respiratory immediately takes over by placing an Ambu bag (artificial manual breathing unit) connected to a mask (used to force air into the patient's lungs by squeezing the inflatable bag) with 100% oxygen over Belinda's face, alternating with chest compressions. Colleen was then relieved of administering chest compressions by one of the medical interns.

The team works effortlessly on Belinda with rescue methods for over thirty minutes. After four rounds of administered medications, the chief peers over at the cardiac monitor and thinks as she shakes her head in dismay, ***Shit, she's still asystole. The sitter said that she was alone in the bathroom for over thirty minutes before she became suspicious and worried, and only then did she look in on her. She was probably hypoxic for more than twenty minutes before the code was even called. Unfortunately, she never had a chance.***

> "OK, OK, everyone.
> Let's call it.
> Time of death is 1355."

Slowly, the team disbands, leaving Colleen and Denise to administer the final care of all, post mortem care to Belinda.

After they are done and satisfied with Belinda's appearance, but leaving in place certain items requested by the investigators, Colleen opens up the window slightly and thinks, *Your spirit is free now Belinda. You can go home.* She shakes her head again as she remembers what Belinda's sitter reported to her, *It seems as though Belinda had a visitor earlier this morning from a supposed boyfriend. That is probably where she received whatever it is she overdosed on. There is definitely going to be a full investigation about this. She is a ME case now. RIP Belinda. I understand that you have been in and out of drug rehab for the past twenty years or so; so sad.* Dr. Barnum shuffles through her chart first before she notifies the next of kin of Belinda's sudden demise, *Hmm, it says here that her sister Sandra is her next of kin.*

> "Ah… hello, my name is Dr. Jeannie Barnum from the hospital.
> May I please speak with Sandra Morgan?"

Feeling a pang of concern over this call, Sandra sits down on her couch before she finds the strength to answer,

> "Hello, yes, this is Sandra.
> Is there something wrong with my sister?
> Is Belinda OK?"

Jeannie intentionally clears her throat before she continues speaking, *Oh, how I hate doing this part of my job,*

> "I am so very sorry to have to inform you about this.
> Your sister Belinda…
> …she has taken a turn for the worse.
> She has …"

Sandra blocks out everything else after hearing those words and she thinks back to life growing up with Belinda. *My God, my baby sister is gone now. Life was not so easy for us, and Belinda was always so impressionable and so very naïve growing up. That is why she got into trouble. She trusted everyone she met. She got hooked up with all of the wrong people, and that was her downfall from there on. I am so heartbroken over this, but at the same time kind of relieved. It feels wrong thinking this but, yes, I am relieved. For more than twenty years now she has lied about everything, stolen from all of us, and she just could not escape from those people and the poison they fed her. She robbed mommy countless times of money, appliances, jewelry and just about everything mom had. She promised over and over again that she would get clean. Then she would steal everything she could carry out of the door and sell everything for some more drugs. Oh, Jehovah, please forgive me, but I think she is better off now. She has suffered so much and caused so much suffering, too. I know that it was ultimately the drugs and not her.* She suddenly hears a voice coming from the telephone and then realizes that she was just off somewhere else,

> "Hello, hello, Sandra?
> Are you still there?
> Sandra, are you still there?"

> "Ah... Oh, yes.
> Sorry.
> Sorry, Dr. Barnum.
> I'm still here."

Dr. Barnum sighs before she replies,

> "Your sister will be sent to the medical examiner's shortly for an autopsy.
> You can go there to see her if you like.
> I can give you the address.
> I am not sure how much you heard of what I said before,
> but we believe your sister overdosed on something that was given to her from a young man who visited her earlier.

I am sure that someone from the authorities will be speaking with you sometime today.

I know that this is a lot for you to grasp right now.

So, please, if you have any questions at all, do not hesitate to call me.

Again, I am so sorry for your loss."

Sandra barely comprehended what the doctor was explaining to her only a few moments ago, but she graciously thanked her before ending the call. After the initial shock of losing her sister, Sandra found herself thinking of what she should say to her mother and siblings.

Belinda was only thirty-nine when she inhaled her final breath. Although her immediate family anticipated one day this day would eventually take place, her senseless death still devastates them to this day. Sandra thinks, *We are no longer three sisters. We are now two. How sad. My sister lost everything because of her addiction to drugs until it finally took the only thing she had left, her life.* Ironically, her boyfriend who visited Belinda in the hospital was found a few days later deceased from a fatal drug overdose.

***

The U.S. flag is observed at half-mast in front of the hospital grounds on Monday morning as we mourn our coworker, friend and colleague, Adam Flores. His young life ends early on a Sunday morning as he heads home from his place of employment. By chance or by fate, Adam witnesses a colleague in distress as she was being abducted outside of the employee parking lot. Without hesitation or fear for his own life, Adam responds to her aid which eventually results in his own demise.

Although her life was spared because of Adam's bravery, Mirna's emotional pain outweighs her physical injuries on that bitter cold morning as she tearfully recalls almost daily, *I can never describe or express how distraught I am over what occurred on that early Sunday morning. It is because of Adam Flores that I am here today. I really did not know Adam personally. We worked in the same building and on the same shift. Our paths may have crossed previously in the cafeteria or in the elevator, and possibly along the hallways of work, but on that specific morning, I believe God placed him there at that particular moment because he became my savior. He acted and reacted without fearing for his own life because someone else was in trouble. I happened to be that someone on that dreadful morning. Normally, I would never leave work at that time. One of my coworkers agreed to relieve me early on that morning so that I may attend early mass. I owe my life to Adam. I am so very sorry for the family he leaves behind; his wife and newborn baby. He was not only our beloved friend and colleague, but he was also a husband, father, son and brother. We have all suffered such a tremendous loss when Adam took his final breath that dreadful, dreadful morning.*

The entire ordeal left Mirna emotionally scarred for a lifetime. She sustained and recovered from a host of physical injuries; including a dislocated left shoulder, right fractured humerus, (long bone of the upper arm) and permanent nerve damage to both of her hands. Because of her injuries, she was no longer able to work in her field, forcing her to an early retirement.

***

All of his external wounds healed and Old Charley O'Connor was eventually placed into a long-term care facility in another state. Mentally, he continued to decline daily. His facility eventually notified the hospital that after six months, Charley succumbed to the effects of his liver disease.

***

The Vincente family behaved themselves for the rest of Mary's hospitalization. She was eventually released home after spending a month in the hospital. Unfortunately, after being home for two months, Mary passed away at home in her sleep.

***

After six long arduous months of recuperating in the hospital and three months of regaining her strength inside of a rehabilitation center, Mrs. Sing was finally discharged home. She became extremely unhappy and depressed because of the changes in the appearance of her skin related to the disease process from Steven Johnson Syndrome, but after time she was extremely grateful to be alive. After long consideration and therapy, Mrs. Sing and her family gained a new perspective on life in general. She and her daughter Lena became huge advocates in the education of the disease that almost took her life.

***

Danny Jones' reattached digit healed well, but he never regained feeling in the affected finger. After his recovery, Danny decided a career change was a necessary move for him. He realized how his own fate could have had a different outcome. Although he rationalized to himself, *It was just my finger. I would have probably survived either way, but I am very fortunate. I saw how hard everyone worked to save my finger for me. This unfortunate mishap opened up my eyes to a world of dedication and compassion that I never knew even existed. I had no choice but to sit around the sidelines and watch everyone work hard to save, comfort and make a difference in another life that they had no connection to at all, other than work. Oh, my job is an important necessary job in our society, but I didn't have a clue as to what it actually takes to do what they do in medicine every single day.* After a year from his hospital discharge date, Danny enrolled into nursing school and is currently working as a nurse practitioner in the field of plastic surgery.

***

Through hard work, determination, and a strong will to live, Lila Johnson survives her physical and emotional damages inflicted upon her, despite all of the odds that had been stacked up heavily upon her in the fire. She lived and cried for many, many long months in the burn unit. During that time, Lila endured multiple painful and extensive surgeries, including skin grafting, blood transfusions, tissue scarring, physical rehabilitation, speech therapy, occupational therapy, psychological evaluations and so much more in order to relearn everything once again. Most importantly, she learned to live and survive despite the tragedy that meant to take her life along with her mother's. Today, Lila travels extensively around the country as an educational and motivational speaker.

***

Carla immediately perks up as her eyes widen significantly with curiosity before she asks,

> "Would you do it again?
> If you could do it all over again,
> would you still become a nurse?"

Carla returns to her seated position and sits back anxiously awaiting her answer. Lydia and Ellie sit quietly as Carla spoke, and then all eyes are patiently focused on to Angela. Her head tilts up as she thinks, *Hmm. Would I do it all over again? Well, I am not so sure. I absolutely loved what I did; my patients, my colleagues, and the endless knowledge that kept filling my tool-*

belt. It was always so extremely satisfying helping others to heal both physically and emotionally. The changes in the medical field are vast, innovative and sometimes alarming, but there is always something new to learn, grasp and explore. I can still recall attending a certain physician's medical rounds quite often. He was very well known in his field and throughout the hospital, but equally feared by most interns and residents. It was an extreme fear of being humiliated during rounds if they were unprepared and not up to date on their patient's overall condition, lab value results and testing. But what I remember most and respect of this particular physician was his compassion and genuine concern for all patients. During his rounds he used to say, "Death is one thing that is promised to us all regardless of race, religion, or station in life. We all will eventually die one day regardless of our social standing. So most importantly, if you learn anything at all from me, I hope that you remember it is our job as medical professionals to treat and care for the living with the utmost respect, compassion, dedication, and to the very best of our ability, regardless of their race, religion, or station. They are all our living patients, and that includes following up on lab and test values." Angela scratches her head as she remembers something else, *Ah… the politics. Oh, yes, I absolutely hated the politics. Realistically, supporting a family is extremely difficult on a nurse's salary that is actually on the frontline of the trenches. No one can ever accuse a nurse of becoming a millionaire on her salary alone.* She sits up tall within the comfort of her seat, takes a deep breath and responds,

"Looking back now,
perhaps if I had some insight beforehand,
I would do it all again… but differently.
It was all so very exciting and heartwarming being a
bedside nurse.
I was at the bedside for so many, very long years because I truly loved it,
but during those years, I never realized that I was be-

coming *Burnt out.*

Unfortunately, it happens.

I loved nursing so very much, but I also enjoyed teaching and the law as well.

I used to say, I don't know how to do anything else, but that was obviously not true.

We are all capable of accomplishing anything and everything, if we try.

So, if I could do it all over again, I would probably leave the bedside after maybe ten years or so to pursue a field involving those three things that I love dearly; nursing, teaching and the law.

It is a little late for me now, but the three of you have such a great, long future ahead of you to enjoy and explore.

The best advice I can give to you now is; Do what you love and love what you do, and that will make you a happy and satisfying career."

Agnes Varona Oquendo, RN, Author is a native New Yorker who has worked many years as a nurse in a clinical setting and then as an educator. She describes her most vital life role as mother and now grandmother, most notably known to her immediate family as MiMi. As a longtime strong advocate for women, health and education, it inevitably drew her attention to becoming an avid long distance runner and athlete, loving and learning a humbleness for the sport. But after a cancer diagnosis and hurdling over life's challenges, she rekindled her lost love for writing, leading her to a new life role as an Indie Author. Agnes' first published book, "Running Against Cancer," became available through Amazon in 2018. In 2019 she published "My Shorts" and "Dark Whispers of a Serial Killer." Her fourth and newest book, "Nurse Diaries," became available in 2020, as she works on book five, while enjoying every moment with her family.

I was the little girl who spent her weekends inside the walls

*of the local Public Library reading, dreaming, exploring and
traveling the world through pages and pages of books.*

*Please help support my beyond adult dreams with just a few words
by leaving a review on Amazon and/or Goodreads for my books.*

Thank you.

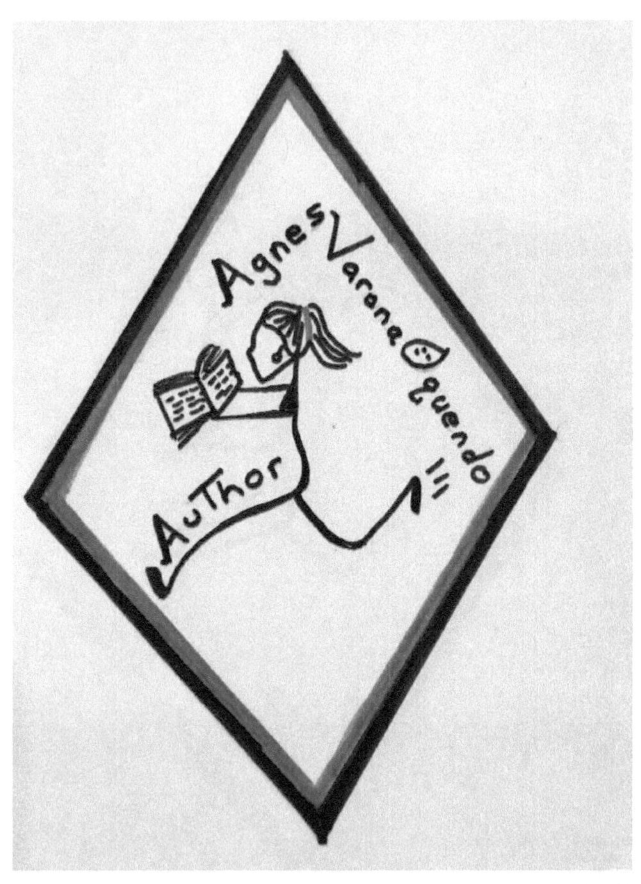
Agnes Varane Oquendo
Author
!!!